Sir Edric's

By Thaddeus

ISBN 978-1-291-62805-0

Dedicated to my first hound, who was a loyal friend all her life long

Herald of Doom

It took all of Edric's knightly discipline to avoid shrieking in terror when the thunderous hammering on his door interrupted his carnal rendezvous. When the herald bellowed for him to answer the door on pain of death he started to curse, until the woman underneath him gave him a slap.

"Just answer the bloody door!" she hissed.

It's all very well for you. It won't be your head, and the gods know what else, they'll chop off.

Adultery was frowned upon in the domains of King Lawrence, and adultery with Lawrence's wife especially so. It wasn't Sir Edric's fault that she was so stunningly beautiful, and so helplessly attracted to handsome, charming knights. Besides, he could hardly refuse her advances; it would've been treason. Engaging in regular episodes of rumpy-pumpy with the Queen was his patriotic duty.

Nevertheless, he hurriedly dressed, paused briefly to enjoy one last look at Her Royal Hotness, and went downstairs before the herald broke down the door.

Sir Edric composed himself, opened the door and stepped outside. "What the bloody hell do you want at this time of night?" he demanded. The fury was not entirely feigned. He loathed heralds. They always brought bad news: tales of pestilence leaving thousands dead, a new royal son permitting the extortion of gifts from every knight in the kingdom, or the return of his wife.

The herald swallowed nervously, and his eyes darted to the sword at Sir Edric's side. "M-my apologies for awaking you, Sir Edric, but the King summons your presence urgently."

"What for?"

The herald shrugged.

"Fine, fine, lead on," Edric commanded, after locking his door. At least he hadn't been arrested and executed. Yet.

The night is young. Not unlike the King's lady wife…

King Lawrence's castle was grand and impressive, and absolutely freezing at night. Edric began to wish he'd paused to put on a thick cloak, like the one the herald had, until he remembered the herald was a peasant and requisitioned the garment for his more important knightly person. Watching the herald shiver and goosebumps crawl over his skin brought a smile to Edric's face.

The delightfully cold herald led him to the throne room, which boded ill. Lawrence was too soft, but at least he was generally amiable and informal. The throne room was only used for serious matters, such as jubilee celebrations, royal weddings, or the execution of men who had enjoyed frisky time with the King's wife.

Edric smiled farewell at the herald, who scowled back at him, and then entered the cavernous chamber. Thick carpets silenced his footsteps as he approached the throne. Either side of him fluted marble columns soared, half-hidden by enormous red banners bearing the King's standard. The King was sitting upon his throne, and not another soul was in attendance. That seemed very strange.

Where's Malthus? Or Drayton? The King doesn't wipe his own backside without asking their advice.

Sir Edric approached the throne until he was ten paces distant, and then went down on one knee and averted his eyes.

"You sent for me, Highness?"

The King sighed. "Yes. And do get up." Edric did so, and his lord and master continued, "What I have to say to you is absolutely secret. Swear upon the sacred bond of liege and vassal that you shall utter no word of it to another."

Huzzah! I live to see another day!

"I swear by the sacred bond of liege and vassal that I shall utter no word of it to another," Edric lied.

"My sceptre and seals have been stolen," the King confessed, his face scrunched up as though he were about to cry.

Edric nodded and waited for the King to recover and go on.

2

"Thieves broke into the treasury last night and stole the serpent sceptre and royal seals that have been handed down from one monarch to another for centuries. Without them, I can make no decrees, enact no new laws and declare no wars."

That explains why the Lords Chamberlain and Chancellor are not present. But why me?

"Dreadful news, Highness," Edric said.

King Lawrence, teary-eyed, nodded wanly. "There is a ransom note. One hundred thousand solidi."

"Bloody hell!" Edric exclaimed, forgetting himself for a moment. One hundred thousand solidi was enough to buy half the kingdom.

The King swallowed back tears and took a moment to compose himself. "I cannot refuse. The law dictates that the holder of the seals and sceptre *is* the King. So, I shall dispatch the army to escort wagons laden with gold to meet the scoundrel and pay for the return of the priceless treasures."

A nagging doubt started to trouble Sir Edric. "So… what do you want me to do, Highness? Lead the wagons?"

Please yes. Pretty please. I could steal my own weight in gold and there'd be so much left nobody would even notice.

"No." The King cruelly dashed his avaricious aspiration. "The wagons will take a long time to make the journey. Before they do so, it's my intention that you shall mount a heroic rescue of the treasures!"

Marvellous. Bloody marvellous.

"I would be honoured, Highness," Sir Edric replied, looking as honoured as a man who'd just taken a mace to the codpiece. "Might I ask who the thief is, and where he is to be met?"

Like a ray of sunshine bursting through an overcast sky, King Lawrence's tormented face was suddenly lit up by a smile. "The Unholy Temple of Despair and Certain Doom. I'm afraid we don't know the identity of the thief, or thieves."

Sir Edric coughed. "And who else shall I take on this epic and incredibly dangerous journey, Highness? A company of Royal Guards, perhaps?"

King Lawrence beamed. "No, just you. And your manservant, if you wish."

He knows...

***

Sir Edric left the throne room, and the disturbingly happy monarch, and hurried home through the chill night. He moved with the dextrous silence of a squirrel in slippers, for the King's wife was a light sleeper and, sadly, he had no time to satisfy her lusty urges. The door did not creak as he opened it, nor did he light lamp or candle. Nevertheless, the moment he closed the door he found himself pounced upon by a naked assailant who tore at his clothes and kissed every morsel of bare flesh she could find.

"Look, Highness, I am afraid I have an urgent matter that I must attend to," he said.

Her Royal Hotness giggled. "You most certainly do. Take your trousers off."

Ah, yet another terrible dilemma. Such is the burden of knightly duty.

"No, no, I really do have something that must be done at once," he insisted, though she continued to lavish him with kisses and the occasional bite. Sir Edric sighed.

Has it come to this? Demanding an insatiable and delectable young lady stop *trying to get me into bed? O, woe is me!*

He grabbed her wrists and pinned her roughly against the wall. That got her attention, he noted with satisfaction. "I must visit my servant, for he has a task to do of utmost importance. Until then, wait in the bedchamber."

She licked her lips and nodded. "I do love it when you take control, Eddy."

4

Sir Edric released his wanton woman, clicked his fingers and pointed upstairs. She obediently went towards the bedroom, and he paused briefly to give her a smart slap on the backside before heading down into the cellar.

"Dog! Where are you?" he shouted. His voice echoed around the vast cellar, which was crammed with bottles of wine and other delights. It was also where Dog, his faithful manservant, lived.

"Here I am, sir," Dog replied. He was sitting at a small table, reading a book and drinking some wine.

Sir Edric sat down and helped himself to Dog's glass of wine. "Terrible news, I am afraid. We face a dangerous journey, and a task of immense peril and woe."

Dog put down the book and asked, "Indeed, sir. Could you elaborate?"

"We are running away, Dog. Somehow the King has discovered I have cuckolded him and now he conspires to send us both on a task that can optimistically be described as suicidal. Therefore, we flee at once!"

To his credit, Dog appeared unperturbed by the news of mortal danger and imminent flight.

"Very well, sir. Obviously I shall pack away money and jewels, but should I seek to take all we can, or sacrifice some material goods for speed?"

Sir Edric pondered that a moment. "Speed is of the essence, I think. A good horse for each of us, and as much gold and jewellery as we can fit into the panniers."

"I see, sir. And your wife?"

Just when I think he's intelligent...

"Don't be stupid, Dog. For a start, she's not in the city. Is she?" he asked, suddenly realising he had no idea what corner of the world was poisoned by Esmerelda's presence. Dog shook his head. "And why would I want to escape one embittered old creature who wants to kill me just to take a second with me?"

5

"I do apologise, sir, I was wondering whether you might want a letter sending to inform her of your plight."

Sir Edric replied, "Of course not! Have the horses saddled and our provisions ready for the earliest hours of the morning. We shall ride east before the sun rises and leave our crowned antagonist far behind us. Now, I have to go and ensure that royal relations are not entirely soured."

He left the mundane tasks in the safe hands of Dog, and returned to his bedchamber where he was set upon by a viciously affectionate young lady.

***

Sir Edric would miss the Queen. She was the perfect blend of lust and beauty, and showed no desire to fritter away time on soppy romantic gestures when they could instead be engaging in rumpy-pumpy. On the other hand, if he remained he would lose his head, and there were plenty more women in the world.

Few so beautiful, or liberal-minded in the bedroom, though...

The knight and his bondsman left his house when the world was still dark, and were riding along at a leisurely pace when a sudden cry halted their progress.

"Sir Edric!" a woman called.

He turned and saw an attractive young woman with long, golden hair and a pleasingly short dress approaching.

"Alas, dear lady, I have no time to spend enthralled by your charms for I am on an important quest," he told her.

"Do I look like a bloody prostitute?!"

Sir Edric ran his eye over her once again. "Yes, and a deliciously expensive one at that but, alas, I have no time to spare." He began to ride away but she seized the reins of Temper, one of his finest horses, to stop him.

He was about to rebuke her insolence, but found, to his distress, that his voice had abandoned him. It was then that he noticed the points of her ears protruding through the golden threads of her hair.

An elf. Super. At least she hasn't shrivelled my cullions to raisins.

"My name," she said, speaking with the slow grandeur and self-importance common to all the pointy-ears, "is Lysandra."

Unable to speak, he raised his hands to indicate he had no idea who she was, and looked to Dog.

As ever, his manservant was well-informed. "A sorceress in the service of King Lawrence, sir. Renowned for being the youngest lady ever to attain the rank, I believe."

Oh, goody. Perhaps the King decided it was best to simply have me murdered. One can only hope she will choose to kill me through sexual exhaustion.

A pretty smile briefly decorated her face as she looked at Dog, but it died the moment she turned her attention back to Sir Edric. "The King has asked me to accompany you both on your quest, to lend you aid and ensure that you do not inadvertently go the wrong way."

To his relief, the knight found his voice restored. "No need, good woman. Dog and I are seasoned men who have travelled far and wide. Are we not, Dog?"

"Indeed, sir."

Lysandra sighed. "I was being polite. The King thinks you'll try to run off because you're a craven traitor. Happily, His Royal Highness can rest easy knowing that should you try..." her voice trailed off and she nodded at a nearby starling.

The bird exploded in a shower of feathers that rained down upon Sir Edric. He brushed the feathers from his shoulder and reconsidered his travelling arrangements.

The journey north would be protracted and dangerous. Plenty of opportunities to escape or perhaps even seduce this elven temptress. She's feisty, but really rather attractive. I wonder how old she is? Maybe I should-

"Sir Edric, are you going to say something, or just stare at me all night?" Lysandra rudely interrupted his cogitation.

She could do with a gag, though. Bloody obnoxious to interrupt a chap when he's thinking.

"I have considered your words, and reluctantly agree to take you with us. We shall return at once to my stables and pick out a steed for you."

The elf pouted. "We should wait until the morning."

Sir Edric shook his head. "Heroic deeds wait not for the sun, my elven enchantress. Dog and I are too fired with patriotic fervour to delay carrying out our lord and master's orders, are we not, Dog?"

"Indeed, sir."

The knight smiled. "So, we can get you a horse and leave together, or Dog and I can trot away without you."

Naturally, the sorceress could hardly refuse and, after a brief detour to the arcane quarter of the city so that she could get her things, they made their way to Sir Edric's stables.

Ah, horses. So much more trustworthy than women, and more reliable than men. A horse would never have divulged my dalliance with the King's wife.

Being a knight of some means he had a score of horses, from Moloch, his monstrous warhorse, to Churl, his most contemptible nag. It soon became apparent that Lysandra knew absolutely nothing of steeds when she approached Moloch and the destrier almost bit her face off.

After some discussion she eventually settled upon Hamilton's Trousers as her preferred steed. Dog saddled the horse, and Sir Edric helped the evidently inexperienced rider up. Her dress, already pleasingly short, rode even higher, exposing her splendid thighs for all to see.

Perhaps having her with us won't be entirely bad news.

***

8

They rode through the night and well into the day, pausing only to eat. Soon they passed the farmland that surrounded the city and reached the rich forests where the nobility hunted and poor people were forbidden to enter.

"My legs are killing me," Lysandra complained for the twenty-third time.

Sir Edric, endowed with legs trained for fitness by the endless riding of both women and horses, was bemused by the sorceress' weakness.

"Surely you ride often?" he asked.

She shot him a venomous glare, though he had no idea why.

"We live and work in a bloody tower! Do you think I gallop up spiral staircases and trot through the library? On the rare occasions I get to leave, tradition dictates I walk."

Ah, tradition, guardian of the ineffable and ridiculous.

"Dog, fetch some filseed oil," he commanded.

The manservant obediently searched through their saddlebags until he found a small jar, which he handed to his master.

"This is splendid stuff for easing aches and pains, particularly riding sores," Sir Edric explained. It had been years since he had used the stuff. On himself, at least.

"Oh… thank you," the sorceress said, seemingly amazed at his kind thought.

"So, if you'd just come over here I'll rub it into your thighs and after mere moments you'll be feeling much happier."

And so will I.

The fleeting smile that had made her face even prettier died beneath the withering gaze she fixed upon him.

This may not end as well as I had hoped.

"I am not some desperate wench to be groped and mauled!" she shouted, snatching the jar from his hands.

Sir Edric raised his hands, hoping by immediate surrender to prevent her unleashing a magical malady upon his person. "I do apologise, it's simply much easier to have someone else do the rubbing."

"I am quite capable of giving myself a rubbing!"

Sir Edric's knightly self-discipline was insufficient to prevent him raising an eyebrow, though he managed to stop a smile spreading across his face.

Lysandra put her hands on her hips. "You know what I mean."

The effort to keep a straight face almost strained his facial muscles.

"I'm going off into the woods. If I see you trying to creep up on me I swear you shall regret it."

And with that cheery promise hanging in the air she stomped away deeper into the forest, leaving Sir Edric and Dog sitting by their horses.

It's rather tempting to flee the harridan, but it's hard to move swiftly in a forest. Better leave it until nightfall.

"Bit odd, isn't it, sir?" Dog asked.

Sir Edric nodded. "Certainly is, Dog. Why on earth would a woman *not* want me to rub oil into her aching thighs? Perhaps excessive use of magic has caused her some sort of brain damage."

His manservant coughed politely. "Indeed, sir, but I was actually referring to her presence here at all. It seems rather irrational. If King Lawrence wants you dead, why send a companion, particularly one so powerful?"

Hmm. That is a good question.

"Lawrence always was a bit of a bed-wetter. Perhaps he's had a change of heart? Sending a chap off to get killed is the act of a rotter, not a weak-kneed fellow."

"Perhaps the Queen interceded on your behalf, sir?" Dog suggested.

Now that *makes sense. If I end up dead she'll have to make do with that limp creature. She's bound to want the return of my sceptre more than his.*

After a suspiciously long time Lysandra returned and Sir Edric took the opportunity to ask precisely what she had been commanded to do.

"I'm to see you safe and sound to the Unholy Temple of Despair and Certain Doom, but you must go in by yourself," she told him.

"Why?"

Lysandra sighed. "Because mages are not permitted to enter, of course. Surely a knight should have learnt this from his tutors?"

Perhaps, but at least I learnt to avoid lecturing people.

"Quite right, dear Lysandra. I do apologise for my ignorance."

***

Fortunately the filseed oil worked well on the elf's magnificent thighs and she did not utter another word of complaint as they travelled north. The road was rather poor, and as night fell they had yet to emerge from the forest. Whilst Dog busied himself erecting the tents, gathering firewood and making the evening meal Sir Edric went into the woods to alleviate himself. On the way back from helping to fertilise the forest he climbed one of the trees to get a better view, and was pleased that no settlement was within sight.

Come nightfall I, and perhaps Dog, shall be away from our fate and the cold beauty who seeks to bind us to it.

He returned to the camp but paused when he heard his two companions chattering.

"I had heard a ridiculous rumour that he was having an affair with the Queen. Do you know anything about that?" Lysandra asked.

"I am afraid," Dog said with a sigh, "that my lips must remain sealed."

Unlike the Queen's.

Before the conversation could progress Sir Edric strode from the forest into the clearing where they had made camp and was pleased to see Lysandra looking a little abashed.

"Hurry up, Dog. Those tents won't put themselves up, will they?" he asked.

Dog, having built the fire, cooked and served the meal, and put up two of the three tents, obediently moved a little faster.

Sir Edric sat by Lysandra and asked, "So, how are your legs?"

"They're much better, thank you."

He ran his eyes over them to judge for himself.

Indeed, they remain splendid. I shall miss them, but my head is worth more than an elf's thighs.

The sorceress was, as he had hoped, tired from riding all night and all day, and soon fell into a deep sleep.

"Opportunity to evade our dreadful doom presents itself, faithful Dog. I shall ride forth. If she awakens shortly thereafter tell her that I heard brigands and went to confront them. If she stays asleep, leave behind all the tents and so on and bring both horses with you."

"Indeed, sir."

Sir Edric mounted Temper and trotted away until he had put a little distance between himself and the camp. However, the moment he burst into a gallop he heard the screams of men and the clang of metal on metal. He dismounted, and proceeded on foot to assess the situation.

On the road ahead was a cart laden with human prisoners, bound and gagged. An Ursk stood on the road, or, to be more precise, with one foot on the road and the other on the skull of a human. Even in the moonlight his elongated canines, great height and dark red skin marked him out as a savage.

Wait a moment...

Sir Edric stood up, brushed the dirt from his raiment and strode confidently down to meet the Ursk.

"Good evening," he called to the warrior.

The Ursk looked up from his prey and squinted as if his eyes told him lies. Sir Edric suddenly recalled just how similar all the Ursk appeared.

Dear gods above, please let this not be a terrible mistake.

"Edric! Edric, thank the gods!" the human, who apparently was still alive, cried.

Sir Edric frowned. "I was talking to the Ursk."

The savage peeled back its purple lips to bare its teeth. The long canines were akin to a lion's, and the two species shared a similar attitude towards mankind.

"Good evening, Edric," Orff No-Balsac eventually replied.

Sir Edric laughed with relief that the Ursk was indeed the lunatic he had met in the dim and distant past. "Slaving are we, Orff?"

The Ursk shrugged. "Mostly slaves, but I'll have a few for supper. Looking to buy one?"

Though his face was half-buried in the dirt of the road the man beneath Orff begged, "For pity's sake, Edric, buy my freedom!"

Orff took his foot off of the man's skull, which was now engraved with several claw marks, and seized him by the scruff of the neck. The Ursk held him up for Sir Edric to inspect.

"Do you know this human, Edric?"

He looks awfully familiar. Ah, sweet fate finally hands me some good fortune!

"I'm John Bellman!" the slave/supper exclaimed. "We've known each other for more than a decade!"

Sir Edric stroked his beard thoughtfully. "Don't I owe you money?"

Confusion and then rage distorted Bellman's face. "You owe me a thousand solidi, as you well know!"

Ah, John. So careful with your purse yet so loose with your tongue. You daft sod.

"Never seen him before in my life," Sir Edric cheerfully informed Orff.

Bellman struggled in the Ursk's iron grip, but was helpless to resist as he was bound, gagged and tossed in the cart with the others Orff had captured.

"By the way, I should probably warn you that there's a vicious, dangerous woman only a mile or so to the south. You might want to get going before she arrives."

Orff nodded. "Your wife?"

"No, an elf sorceress. You don't want to be here when-"

"Stop right there, you vile animal!" Lysandra's unmistakably pompous voice rang out in the darkness.

Sir Edric turned and saw her and Dog on horseback. "I say, that's a bit unfair."

"I was talking to the Ursk," she replied. "What are you doing here, foul creature?"

I bet Orff is thinking much the same.

"I was taking prisoners when brave Sir Edric here approached," the Ursk said.

You sly devil.

"Known to all Ursk from his blood-soaked victory at Hornska, Sir Edric commanded that I cease and desist from my evildoing and at once release those whom I had bound. I was just about to let them go when you arrived," Orff said, attempting to smile and instead baring his razor-sharp fangs like a hungry tiger.

Astonishment stole the words from Lysandra's mouth at the Ursk's explanation.

Sir Edric beckoned Dog to come closer. "Climb into the cart and cut free those poor souls, victims of this horrible beast!" he ordered. "Except John Bellman. Leave him in there and make sure his gag's tight," he muttered under his breath.

Dog gave a nod of obedience and did as he was told.

"Well, that's as it should be," Lysandra acknowledged. "Well done, Sir Edric," she said, the words struggling from her lips as though reluctant to be spoken.

Bah. I've saved a score of souls, but my own remains imperilled.

"And as for you," she said, pointing at Orff No-Balsac, "Begone from this place and promise never to return!"

"I promise by all the gods to never return."

I wonder if she knows that the Ursk are atheists?

"Very well. Off with you!" she commanded in the haughty tone of a woman who both enjoyed and was accustomed to being obeyed.

Apparently not. Ha, not so well-educated as she likes to think.

Orff winked at Sir Edric, bowed theatrically to Lysandra and studiously avoided going anywhere near Dog. The Ursk clambered aboard his cart and set it trundling off into the night.

"Should I have slain him?" Lysandra wondered.

No, he's a friend of mine. Admittedly, he kills and eats people, but we all have our little flaws. Besides, most of them are only peasants.

"How can a creature repent from wickedness if they are dead?" Sir Edric asked, recalling one of the pretentious questions a priest in his childhood had been fond of repeating.

For the second time that night the sorceress appeared at a loss for words.

"Perhaps there is more to you than I first thought," she finally said.

Sympathy! The first step on the staircase to the bedroom!

A Decaying Friendship

"How fares your training?" Lysandra asked.

Sir Edric smiled in answer and Dog smacked him in the face with a quarterstaff. The knight fell onto his back and almost passed out. Lysandra placed a hand on his head and the pain eased.

"Things always go wrong when women interrupt," Sir Edric complained. Dog had reported that the elf needed barely thirty minutes of sleep last night, meaning that escape whilst she slept would prove nigh on impossible. He had hopes of evading his deadly quest, but until he could actually concoct a new plan it seemed wise to sharpen up his prowess by sparring with his annoyingly proficient manservant. His martial edge had become blunted by easy living in the capital.

The elf raised a perfectly plucked eyebrow.

He tossed his staff to Dog. "Ready our trusty steeds," he ordered.

When his manservant had gone Lysandra folded her arms and looked at him.

"I seem to recall you growing irritated when *I* stared at you," he complained, wiping some of the sweat from his forehead.

"I'm simply trying to understand your sudden interest in training."

I can't bloody run away, so I might as well hone my skills.

"Oh? I'm trying to understand why you're so relaxed about escorting a noble knight and his scruffy but nevertheless sound manservant to certain death."

She smiled. "Not certain... merely highly probable. Despite what the King said I heard that, in your youth, you were quite the warrior."

In my youth!? I am *in my bloody youth!*

"I'm only forty-one," he protested.

She laughed. "You're old enough to be my father."

Lysandra was surprised when Sir Edric refused to say she could call him 'daddy'. Before he could rebuke the uppity whippersnapper, Dog returned with the horses. Sir Edric mounted Temper and led the others northward.

**

"Tremble at my prowess, puny adversaries!" Sir Edric bellowed triumphantly.

One of his foes lay dead, a crossbow bolt embedded in its skull. The other pigeons flew away in distress, though he swiftly reloaded and downed one of them in flight.

Dog applauded politely.

As well he should. He might be well-versed in swordplay, quarterstaffs, maces, falchions, axes and spears, but when it comes to shooting I'm second to none.

He slung the crossbow over his shoulder whilst Dog scurried off to fetch the second bird.

"You do realise I could slay them all with fireballs?" Lysandra asked.

I wonder if her superiority complex comes from being a sorceress, or an elf?

He rolled his eyes. "Aye, and you'd burn them all to a crisp. I prefer my meat succulent, not carbonised."

The travellers emerged from the forest early in the morning, and ate their meal by the side of the highway. Merchants and peasant folk wandered by, often pausing to stare at Lysandra.

"Why do they stare so?" she asked Sir Edric. A small gaggle of unwashed peasants had passed them by, and every one had gaped openly at the elf.

Well, you are rather pretty.

"Elves are not common in these parts."

"Elves are not common at all," she replied.

Sir Edric found the pigeon to be delicious, which was no surprise as prey hunted by himself always tasted better than the stuff bought in shops. He was just about to mount Temper when a band of emaciated, dirty people who were barefoot and clad in little but rags shuffled down the road. They surrounded him and fell to their knees, hands clasped in supplication.

Now, where did I put my whip?

"Help us, brave nobleman!" a toothless crone with wisps of grey for hair implored him.

"What has happened to you?" Lysandra asked.

"Our lord is a tyrant, lady," the hag answered. "He works us all the hours of the sun with barely enough food to live, yet he feasts like a king in his grand manor!"

"And not just that," a lanky youth with straw-like hair added. "He's doing foul and unspeakable things. Dabbling in witchcraft and raising the dead!"

There were murmurs of agreement from the other peasants.

"Who is your lord?" Sir Edric asked, though he already had a sneaking suspicion.

"Baron Henry Greymond," the crone answered.

"Of course we shall-" Lysandra began, but Sir Edric cut her off.

"-discuss your predicament."

The three of them wandered a little from the road to converse in private.

"What is there to discuss?" Lysandra asked. "These people have been cruelly maltreated and need our help!"

Sir Edric sighed. "Have you ever heard of the feudal system? Scruffy poor people do boring manual labour to provide income for knights and barons, and we gallop off and fight wars to protect the helpless, harmless peasants. A man's got every right to make his vassals work. I bet they weren't complaining when Henry was killing Ursk and chasing down ogres."

"And the witchcraft? Raising the dead?" Lysandra demanded.

He snorted derisively. "Peasants are always spouting nonsense. I'm surprised they don't claim he's fathered a gerbil." A thought occurred to him, and he added, "Besides which, we have an urgent royal mission to which we must attend. We mustn't keep the King waiting."

To Sir Edric's intense surprise Dog coughed and asked the elven do-gooder to give the two men a moment alone.

"Don't tell me you agree with her."

Dog shook his head. "Not at all, sir. However, if you did go and see Baron Greymond might he not be able to help you escape the journey to the Unholy Temple? A minor dose of poison and a compliant apothecary could give you a mild fever to evade that perilous duty until it's too late and the wagons have reached their destination."

Dog, you clever fellow! Where did you learn such low cunning?

He beckoned the sorceress over and announced that his natural instinct to protect the innocent eclipsed his fondness for feudalism.

Her sparkling green eyes narrowed in suspicion, but she did not demur.

The peasants gave a ragged cheer and then, predictably, asked for some money. Even more predictably, the elf claimed she hadn't brought any.

"Aren't you very rich?" she asked impertinently.

"Yes. I accrued such impressive wealth by the simple expedient of not giving it away at every opportunity," he replied.

A few stavrata prompted only grunts of thanks from the greedy rascals, and the three travellers rode onward to Baron Greymond's manor.

***

The baronial manor had become even more opulent than Sir Edric remembered. A new tower thrust from the earth and pierced the skies, a magnificent monument to modern

19

architecture and defence. Or a subconscious attempt to compensate for something, if the whores of Sir Edric's youth had been telling the truth.

"So, what do you know of this Baron Greymond?" Lysandra enquired.

He's an alcoholic gambler and rancid glutton. Rather handy in a scrap, though.

"He's a vivacious fellow."

Strangely, there was no sign of peasants working the fields around the manor, and when they dismounted outside the front door no grooms came to stable their steeds. Sir Edric cautiously knocked on the door, only to find it swing open on creaking hinges.

This is odd... something's wrong. I smell danger in the air. It is at times such as this that a man experienced in the art of war knows how to proceed.

"After you, Dog," he said, after fetching his crossbow and a quiver full of bolts from Temper.

His manservant nodded and unsheathed his blade before heading inside the manor. Sir Edric followed a moment later, crossbow raised and ready to fire at a moment's notice.

"Hello?" Dog shouted. His voice echoed in the enormous entrance hall, which appeared bereft of life.

A quick search found that the hall was entirely deserted, as was the rest of the manor. Meals had been left half-eaten, but not long ago for even the soft fruit had only just begun to rot. The hearths had gone cold, but none of the tapestries, jewellery or horses had been stolen.

"You know what this means," Lysandra said. The three of them were in the feasting hall, gorging themselves on the food that was still fresh enough to be eaten.

Sir Edric guzzled happily on a bottle of wine. "Just so. Greymond isn't brutalising the poor, because he isn't here. After we rescue the treasures of this manor to prevent them falling into the nefarious clutches of looters we should continue on our way."

The elf put her head in her hands. "No, you bloody idiot! It corroborates what we were told. Greymond probably is doing some vile necromancy, which is both illegal and immoral, and we must stop him!"

Sir Edric scowled at Dog, who was staring at the table and chewing a loaf of white bread.

Damn it, Dog. Now look what you've got us into.

"Of course, that would be my preference, but Greymond's lands are vast, we have no idea where he is and we can't dally long."

"We haven't checked the tower yet."

Bugger.

After they had eaten – or in Sir Edric's case drunk – their fill and he had liberated the manor of its gold and silver they made their way to the tower. It was a round structure, scarred with narrow crosses for crossbow-wielding defenders to use and crowned with crenellations. He knocked on the door, and waited in vain for an answer.

"See? Nobody's home," he told Lysandra. "Now, onward! Royal command dictates we travel with all haste to-"

"Oh, shut up," she interrupted.

Sir Edric and Dog stood to one side and Lysandra closed her eyes momentarily. An instant later she opened her mouth and a bolt of lightning erupted from her lips. The thick oak door exploded in a shower of splinters and the humans' ears rang with the violence of the magic.

Sir Edric peered inside. Spiralling stairs led both up and down.

"I'm sure you know more about dabbling in forbidden magic than me. Would you do it underground or on top of a tower?" he asked.

At Lysandra's suggestion they headed down, Dog leading the way. After some time the manservant came to an iron-studded wooden door. Dog tried opening it, but when he touched the handle a strange hissing sound came from behind them. Sir Edric turned and saw a fog-like miasma flowing down the stairs. His head grew heavy and he slumped to the ground.

***

Drinking three bottles of wine had evidently been a mistake. His head hurt more than when Ganska Gro-Braful had sat on it. His eyes didn't seem to be working either, because when he tried opening them all he saw was a vague blurriness.

"Dog, fetch me some wine," he commanded quietly. Medicinal alcohol was bound to ease his symptoms and fortify his health.

Dog did not reply, so he gave his manservant a gentle kick and discovered the dark, still shape by his side was, in fact, a rock.

Aching head, feeble eyes, and now, quite possibly, a broken foot. All from a few bottles of wine. Perhaps Lysandra's right, and I am getting old.

Old or not, he struggled to his feet and wandered hesitantly forward. His vision was beginning to sharpen and he just about made out the iron bars before he wandered into them.

"I demand to speak to the jailer!" he shouted, wincing at the volume of his own cry, which did nothing to soothe his aching head.

He repeated his demand twice more, and only then did anybody bother to answer.

"Good evening, sir," Dog said, in his unflappable fashion, from a cell to his left.

"Is Lysandra there?" he asked.

The two men waited in expectant silence until, eventually, she answered.

"Yes."

She sounds upset. Probably feels stupid, as well she might, for leading us into this mess.

"Splendid. A smidgen of sorcery to remedy our incarcerated status would go down swimmingly."

"I can't. The fiend bound my hands with electrum manacles and the foul metal has robbed me of my magic! I can't cast anything!" She sighed. "How do you people live like this? Not being able to bend matter to your will or breathe flames? I feel like an insect, not an elf."

Marvellous. Now we're trapped underground and the do-gooding elf has been reduced to the magical equivalent of a eunuch. This is what happens when you try to help peasants.

Unsurprisingly his sword, and Dog's, had been seized, as had his crossbow. The dirks the two men kept in their boots had not been taken, which was a small mercy. Sir Edric fell silent as footsteps, some precise and some dragging, approached.

From the cell on his right he heard Lysandra gasp, and the reason why soon entered his own field of vision. A man, whose skin was a dreary grey, shambled into view and looked at the knight with eyes that were halfway to milky white. Blood dribbled from the corner of its mouth and it uttered a mindless moan. Potent halitosis escaped its lips when it groaned, forcing Sir Edric a little further back into his cell.

Well, at least being raised from the dead hasn't diminished the peasant's intelligence or personal hygiene.

A tall, fat man strolled into view and stopped outside his cell. Baron Henry Greymond appeared much the same as when Sir Edric had met him last. Ruddy-faced, rather bloated and eminently satisfied with himself.

"Edric! Fancy seeing you here. Why did you break into my tower?"

Be wise and subtle, Edric. The slightest slip could mean death, or, worse still, becoming an undead thrall.

"To apprehend you, vile necromancer!" Lysandra answered.

"Wait a moment, that's why *she* came here," Sir Edric said, hoping to repair the damage to the fraying thread of hope, "*I* came here to see my old friend Henry and to quash the scurrilous rumours that you'd become a tyrant."

Greymond stroked his beard with chubby fingers. "This is quite the quandary. I shall have to think about it. Once I have dined I shall return to tell you your fate."

The fat baron walked away, followed by his corpse-thrall. After they heard a distant door click shut and a key turn the three prisoners burst into conversation.

"If he's having dinner that only gives us four, perhaps five hours at the most," Sir Edric predicted. "Now would be an ample time to disclose the cunning plans I am sure you have both been contemplating."

"You might want to say your prayers," Lysandra answered.

Very helpful.

***

The opening door stirred Sir Edric, who had been on the verge of nodding off. Greymond, escorted by four mindless minions, approached the knight's cell.

"Good news!" Greymond said, rubbing his hands together and jangling an over-sized ring of chunky iron keys.

Huzzah! Freedom beckons me like a dockside harlot.

"I'm going to add you to my little army of walking corpses," the necromancer continued. "You and Dog will be useful for your fighting skills," he said, before turning to face Lysandra's cell. "For you I have rather more intimate plans."

Sir Edric could almost hear the elf shuddering.

"Come on, Henry. Are we not old friends? We've both done our fair share of law-breaking in the past, but friends don't betray one another, or brutally murder and then raise the other as an undead thrall."

24

It seemed that the baron was considering Sir Edric's plea, but then he realised the fat necromancer was simply ogling Lysandra.

"Sorry, Eddy, but I can't take the risk. I hope it's some comfort that the kill will be a clean one."

It's about as comforting as a cactus codpiece.

Greymond unlocked the cell door and stepped back to allow his life-impaired underlings to grab Sir Edric's arms and all but drag him out. Their stench was rank and Sir Edric retched as they hauled him after their master. He saw Lysandra kneeling, hands together in prayer. She offered him a sad smile as the undead dragged him to his fate.

Past the locked door was a tunnel that led to a larger chamber carved into a precise hemisphere. Upon the ceiling a glowing chart of the stars had been etched.

Reminds me of the mirrored ceiling in my estate.

In the centre of the chamber was a large stone table daubed with countless bloodstains. Upon it a silver knife rested. Greymond took the knife and gestured at the table. The quartet of corpses, surprisingly strong for men whose muscles were festering, were more than a match for Sir Edric's resistance. They forced him towards the gruesome furniture. Once they reached it they picked him up and roughly dropped him onto it, their rotting hands holding him still. He tried to turn his face away from their foul breath, but the effort was in vain.

Greymond looked rather happy as he loomed over his former friend, knife in hand. "Any final words, Eddy?"

"I'd like to pray, if I may."

The baron's face fell and he frowned, apparently unsure whether the less than devout knight was being serious or taking the piss.

"Honestly?"

"Cross my heart and hope to be ritually sacrificed."

Greymond shrugged, and at that signal the rotting rascals holding Sir Edric's arms let go. He put his hands together for a split second before plunging one into his boot, seizing the handle of his dirk and hurling the blade at the baron. The gods answered his prayer and the blade pierced Greymond's eye. Hideous humour dribbled down his face, the villain fell to a gurgling death, and the grip of the festering fellows holding Sir Edric's legs slackened.

Fear lent him speed and he leapt from the table to retrieve his rather gooey dirk.

"Uuurrrrrgghhhhh…" one of the corpses said.

Sir Edric cut the fat baron's belt and took his keys. He turned and saw all four undead were shuffling towards him. He kicked the nearest one in the leg, and the limb came clean away from its decomposing body. Before the others could reach him he raced back towards the jail and began trying the keys to unlock the door. He happened upon the right one and opened it, but a cold hand seized his wrist.

"Grraargghhh," the undead said.

It moved its free hand towards Sir Edric's eyes, and he instinctively lashed out with his dirk. The sharp blade cut clean through the creature's forearm, and a second slash severed the hand holding his wrist. He sprinted through the doorway, slammed the door shut and locked it to keep the corpses out.

"Sir Edric?! You're alive!" Lysandra exclaimed, sounding astonished and, even better, impressed.

"Huzzah!" Dog loyally cheered, though in his far cell he could not see his master.

"It takes more than a maniac trying to cut my heart out with a dagger to kill the likes of me. Hold your manacles up so I can try the keys."

She did so obediently. As he tried the numerous keys the sound of dead men hammering on the jail door spurred him on. Working feverishly, at length he found the right one and freed her.

Perhaps in happier circumstances she'll let me put manacles on her.

26

She wrapped her fingers around the iron bars and the metal turned to water. Moments later the sorceress freed Dog from his cell, but they remained trapped in the jail, a horde of walking corpses between them and escape.

"Stand back," Lysandra commanded imperiously.

Sir Edric and Dog obediently moved as far behind her as they could, and shielded their eyes as a river of flame surged from her raised hands. In mere moments the thick oak door was reduced to cinders by her magical flames, and the score of creatures beyond were burnt to a crisp. The elf inspected her handiwork, and was satisfied that none had survived.

A peremptory search through Baron Greymond's quarters uncovered their weapons and Sir Edric found several bottles of wine. On the way out Lysandra caused a cave-in to prevent anyone finding their way to the ritual chamber.

When they emerged it was deepest night, and Sir Edric was relieved to see that Temper, Twenty-Six and Hamilton's Trousers remained safe and sound in the stables. The quest demanded speed, but they could not travel day and night without rest. After spending the night in the manor Sir Edric resumed his journey northward towards highly probable death.

A Sudden Malady

It was a rather beautiful summer morning, and still early enough for the three riders to have the road north entirely to themselves. As he rode along, it occurred to Sir Edric that only one thing could make the journey more pleasant. He rummaged around in one of Temper's panniers, until his hand emerged clutching his pipe and tinderbox.

"Sir Edric, smoking is a filthy habit," Lysandra admonished him. "The diabolical fumes of smoke char the lungs and taint the mouth and throat. It's a despicable custom that causes countless diseases."

He laughed. "You do remember I'll probably be dead in a few weeks? Concerns about my health do not trouble me."

"And what about those around you?"

Sir Edric looked around. Within eyeshot the only living creatures were three horses, his manservant, the elf, and a blackbird that was savaging a worm in a field by the side of the road.

"Oh, very well," he conceded. "If the aroma of smoke displeases you so, I grant you leave to return to Awyndel. Dog and I shall accomplish the royal mission without you, never fear."

He prepared to light his pipe, only for a sudden gust of wind to pluck the tinderbox and pipe from his hands. Temper's pannier opened itself and the two objects dropped neatly inside.

"I think not. This shall be a smoke-free quest," Lysandra declared.

Sir Edric sighed. "You know, most elves rather like smoking. Which reminds me, why don't you know how to ride a horse? An elf who can't ride is like a dragon who can't fly."

Lysandra, seated bolt upright atop Hamilton's Trousers, tutted. "And what would a human know of elvenkind? I would wager you've never even been to elven lands."

"I'll have you know that I was a personal guest at Prince Sarpellon's summer home."

She frowned at his words. "That is a most... unexpected claim."

"It's true. The view of the beautiful crystal waters of Lake Rhados will live with me until the day I die."

I was fortunate to be given a cell with a window.

"Anyway," Sir Edric continued, "you're making fine progress with your steed. Just remember to have faith in Hamilton's Trousers, and to treat your horse as you would a servant."

Without the beatings, obviously.

The continual days of riding were clearly making up for her lack of experience on horseback. Although she did not appear entirely comfortable just yet, her complaints of being saddle sore and use of filseed oil had markedly declined.

The day was lovely, as small white clouds sailed serenely through the bright blue sky. Alongside the road was a picturesque lake upon which swans and ducks calmly swam. The sun blazed brightly, and Lysandra looked stunning in the golden rays. Sir Edric surreptitiously cast his eye over her.

I suppose there are worse travelling companions to have.

***

A few days later they arrived at Sir Edric's manor which lay, by chance, on their route to the Unholy Temple. His manor was smaller and more heavily fortified than Greymond's, which the knight attributed to his military forebears. Greenlock, the town that had grown near the manor, was replete with smiths, jewellers and an unusually high proportion of brothels.

As they entered the town they happened upon a pie seller. Lysandra paused and positively gawped at his peculiar appearance.

"What race is he?" she whispered to Sir Edric.

Ah, academia. Marvellous for teaching people what books contain, less useful for telling them what's in the real world.

"A Fyntok. Surely you must have read of them?" he teased her.

She fixed him with her sternest and most pompous expression. Long experience had taught him that whilst women talked too much it was when they became silent that a man needed to become worried, so he answered her quickly.

"A bird-man, in essence. Ostrich-like legs, a thin layer of feathers all over and a beak that's short but strong enough to break through plate armour. No wings, but they can run faster than a horse."

"They sound fearsome," she said, although the Fyntok selling pies did not appear particularly terrifying.

Sir Edric shook his head. "They're actually tremendous cowards and devious, deceitful sorts. But if they're ever forced to fight they're remarkably good at it."

At the elf's behest they approached the Fyntok, whose height on foot more or less matched theirs on horseback.

"How much for three pies for we weary travellers?" Lysandra asked.

The Fyntok twitched his head to the side. "Kree-kree! Six nummi apiece, but for a fair lady I cut the price to five nummi."

"What's in the pies?" Dog asked.

The Fyntok made a strange chirping sound. "Delicious tasty meat! Yum yum!"

"Fifteen nummi for three large pies sounds like suspiciously good value," Sir Edric said. "There isn't any horsemeat in them, is there?"

The Fyntok swore not, but Sir Edric and Dog were unconvinced. Happily Lysandra conjured up a solution.

"This," she said, holding up an unmarked bronze ring, "is a Ring of Truth. He who wears it cannot tell a lie."

The Fyntok reluctantly agreed and slipped the ring upon a feathered finger.

"Is there any horsemeat in the pies?" Sir Edric asked.

"Kree-kree! No. No horsemeat."

So, in exchange for fifteen nummi they bought three large pies, and found, to their delight, that they were as delicious as the Fyntok had promised. About halfway through their meal, which they ate in the saddle, Lysandra remembered she had yet to retrieve the Ring of Truth.

"I do apologise for my suspicious friends," Lysandra said. "Fancy them claiming you were selling us horsemeat."

The Fyntok clashed the mandibles of his beak together noisily. "No horsemeat! Only delicious tasty human flesh. Yum yum!"

Lysandra and Dog spat out the mouthfuls of meat they had been chewing. Astounded by the feathery fellow's revelation, Sir Edric swallowed in shock and tried not to imagine which particular part of human anatomy was sliding down his gullet.

***

After the Fyntok had been placed in stocks in the town square and pelted with a mixture of rotting vegetables, his own pies and copious amounts of horse dung, Sir Edric led Lysandra and Dog to his manor. To his immense relief the poisonous spider to whom he was shackled by marriage was somewhere else. She had evidently returned at some point, however, as he discovered when he visited the master bedroom.

"She's taken down the mirrors!" he exclaimed, staring at the ceiling.

Lysandra sighed. "A mirrored ceiling? That's perverse."

To be fair, if I had a face like Esmerelda's I'd dislike mirrors too.

The elf was shown to her quarters, yet Dog tarried awhile.

"Sir, perhaps I should summon an apothecary?"

Sir Edric frowned. "If you're feeling ill, by all means. Whilst you're doing it, have them send up a pair of whores for me. If

I'm going to highly probable death I want to have at least one happy episode in the story of my demise."

Dog coughed. "An apothecary for you, sir? To tend to the fever which has, by chance, suddenly appeared?"

Sir Edric clicked his fingers. "Ah, yes! Do so at once, Dog. Actually, send the whores first, and *then* summon the apothecary."

After his knightly person had been suitably invigorated by a pair of frisky young vixens Sir Edric got dressed, enjoyed a quick footbath, and then had his manservant bring in the apothecary. The peddler of potions was a stooped old man with so many wrinkles his face looked like a quilt of foreskins. Dog closed the door behind him and Sir Edric explained his particular situation.

"Ah... yes..." the apothecary said, nodding and speaking so slowly the knight feared he would expire of thirst long before the Unholy Temple could claim his soul. "Your man told me... all this. Hmm. Yes." He stopped talking and smiled.

Why are old people so bloody slow? One would've thought that as their end approached they'd become quicker to make the most of their diminishing time.

"Well?" Sir Edric snapped.

His question seemed to stir the ancient apothecary back to wakefulness. A gnarled old hand dove inside his capacious black robes and fished out a small glass vial containing a turquoise liquid.

"This is what you... must drink," the apothecary said, pointing at the turquoise substance in case Sir Edric was incapable of determining that drinking typically involved a liquid.

The apothecary seemed in no hurry to hand it over so Sir Edric snatched the vial, downed its contents and lay back on his bed.

"Splendid. See yourself out. My man will give you a few stavrata for your trouble," Sir Edric ordered.

Excellent. My skin's hot and my head aches already. A few weeks in bed, possibly being nursed by Lysandra, and then I shall be safe. Huzzah!

The elderly man did not move, so Sir Edric repeated himself, more deliberately and loudly. A slow smile crept across the apothecary's face.

"Death to you, vile fornicator and corruptor of women!" the old man said, cackling with glee. "You deflowered my lovely Rachel years ago, and now I kill you to avenge her honour!"

Bloody hell!

"That's a lie," Sir Edric protested, after racking his brains to remember Rachel. "I never deflowered her. She'd been ridden more times than a seaside donkey by the time I got around to her."

Oh gods, the pain!

The apothecary's mouth gaped in shock, at which point the knight cried out for help.

Dog ran in, sword drawn.

"He's poisoned me!" Sir Edric said, his voice already withered to a whisper.

Dog at once swung his sword and decapitated the ancient assassin. The wrinkly head landed in Sir Edric's footbath, splashing cloudy water onto the carpet.

Take that, you murderous swine!

"Tell me the poison, sir, and I shall fetch the antidote at once."

Oh. Damn. It may have been wiser to wait just a minute before lopping the old fool's head off.

"I don't know," Sir Edric murmured.

Dog looked down at the apothecary's severed head and frowned. "I shall bring Lysandra."

The elven enchantress had been in the middle of having a luxurious bath, and ran to Sir Edric's bedchamber rather wet and wearing only a thin shift. The sight perked the knight up somewhat, though his fatigue and pain was such that he lacked the strength to ogle her properly. Fortunately, she rushed to his side, leaned over him to press her hand to his forehead and afforded him a generous view without having to move a muscle.

"What did you eat or drink?" she asked.

Nothing so delicious as elven crumpet...

"I drank a little of a turquoise beverage," he answered. He spoke slowly, partly because his throat was starting to swell and talking hurt, and partly because he was rather enjoying having Lysandra so near.

At last the elf's years of book-reading proved useful. The poison, she asserted with the confidence of a smug mage, was an artificial concoction known as Widow's Fancy. Its symptoms included pain that would rise from a dull ache to violent stabbing, swelling of the throat and nose, and certain death.

"*Certain* death?!" Sir Edric croaked in alarm.

O, woe is me! What have I ever done to deserve such a vile fate?

"Unless we can find the antidote, of course. However, the only known cure is an exceedingly rare flower: the Paramour's Tears."

Dog raised an eyebrow. "Sir, is that not the plant that you and Lady Honeybush found when you took her for a dalliance on the slopes of Mount Nevermore?"

Dog, you genius!

The knight nodded, and winced at the pain such slight movement induced.

"How far away is this Mount Nevermore?" Lysandra asked. "The poison will kill him within two days, perhaps three if I stay behind and ease his symptoms."

I can certainly think of a way you could take my mind off the pain...

"I shall have to embark at once to stand any chance. Gods save you, sir. Farewell, my lady."

34

And so Dog, pausing only to collect the weapons and food he would need, mounted Twenty-Six and rode east to the perilous Mount Nevermore.

***

It soon transpired that Lysandra's list of symptoms was not quite complete. Barely had Sir Edric heard the hooves of Twenty-Six galloping away than his cullions began to swell. In truth, it was a faintly pleasant experience, at first. However, they soon started aching terribly.

Lysandra insisted upon being his nurse, though she had sadly taken the time to dry herself properly and don less revealing attire. Sir Edric asked her to examine his nether regions and she fixed him with a glare so severe he was certain only his obvious agony prevented her from slapping him.

"I know you're ill, Sir Edric, but I'm not going to stand for any of your nonsense."

Oh, gods… ice would be worth its weight in gold.

"At least get me some ice," he pleaded.

"No," she refused, wagging a matronly finger at him when he attempted to speak again. "My memory is entirely correct, and there is no such symptom as you claim. Matthew Carrington's Compendium of Poisons is *the* definitive codex on such matters."

Maybe I've already died, and this is Hell.

Although she refused to probe his tender portions he was grateful that her healing hands alleviated the worst of the swelling from his throat and nose, enabling him to breathe with relative ease. The elf also soothed his pounding head, although the removal of that pain meant that the fiery torment of his trousers soon became the focus of his woe.

"Could I have something to eat?" he asked, his voice rasping.

"What would you like?"

Ice. And I'd like you to present it on a platter of ice, which I shall rest on my groin.

In the end she fetched him some grapes and water, mercilessly denying his entirely reasonable desire for a little wine, and beer, and whisky.

Sleep claimed him after the minuscule meal, and in dreams he found a blessed relief. His mind delivered him into the arms of King Lawrence's wife, and she was suitably relieved to see him safe and sound. Barely had he wrapped his arms around her than she transformed into the horror of Esmerelda. Try as he might to break free her grip was irresistible and she drew nearer-

"Sir Edric! Are you alright?" Lysandra asked, having shaken him so roughly sleep was banished. "You were screaming, and I feared you were having a nightmare."

He smiled wanly. "Thank you for waking me up."

The passage of time was perverse, and seemed disinclined to obey the usual rules. It moved with great haste when he was fearful of imminent death, and then slowed to the most tedious, plodding pace when the stabbing pain pricking his plums was most piercing.

Sir Edric had the curtains pulled back and the windows to his balcony opened, that he might gaze upon the stars.

How many nights did I camp under those beautiful shining stars, on the eve and aftermath of battle? Yet here I lie, vanquished by an angry old git whose daughter was a harlot of the first water.

"Dog will come back," he said, more to himself than Lysandra.

He'd better bloody well come back. If I die he'll become Esmerelda's servant, and he'd have the rough end of that deal.

"Why do you call him Dog?"

He frowned, wondering if he'd heard the elf aright. "That's his name."

Lysandra smiled.

Such a pretty smile. Almost makes up for her pompous self-regard.

"But surely his parents did not name him so?"

This is so unfair. I'm dying and she's wittering on about a peasant, admittedly a useful one, but still. She should be holding me in her arms, whispering sweet nothings in my ear and getting me some sodding ice.

"No. I inherited him from an uncle who died in a freak llama accident. His old name was frankly ridiculous, and entirely unsuited to a man of his lowly station. Could you come and do my throat again, please?"

Lysandra rose from her bedside chair and obediently pressed her hands to his neck. Her hands felt cool, though whether that was because he was hot or elven blood ran cold he knew not.

"It is an unkind name."

"Not so. Are dogs not useful, intelligent and loyal? The name proved well-chosen, for Dog is the finest manservant I have had."

Let us hope that Dog proves as skilled at fetching as his name would suggest.

***

Slumber declined his company during the night, and given the horrific vision of his wife he was not disappointed by the rejection. Lysandra stayed by his side, yet her ministrations gradually became less effective and his throat and nose constricted until he could barely breathe.

In the distance, through his still-open windows, he heard a faint sound. It became louder and he could make out the sound of cheering coming from the town.

Cheering my demise? Those ingrates. Unwashed dullards and empty-headed churls to a man.

The sound of a horse galloping towards the manor came through the windows, and he realised Dog was returning.

Huzzah! My faithful vassals celebrate the deliverance of their beloved lord!

Dog, face redder than a baboon's bottom and coated with sweat, burst through the door and handed a small purple flower to Lysandra.

"Is that it, my lady?" he asked, chest heaving.

If it isn't my last act will be to have you marry a pig.

"Yes," she answered, plucking a single petal, no larger than a fingernail. "Open wide, Sir Edric."

He did so, and she placed the petal upon his tongue. It had a minty taste and, as he lacked the ability to swallow, it began to dissolve on his tongue.

Outside his window the cheering continued and grew louder.

His head became clearer, the passages of his nose and gullet loosened and, best of all, the raging fires of Hell that had once blazed in his trousers were rapidly being extinguished.

"Huzzah for you, Dog," he said.

Dog's face had almost returned to a normal hue, and he bowed his head. "Not at all, sir."

"Help me up."

They're only peasants, but it befits me, as their liege, to show myself recovered to ease their natural concern for my health.

He put one arm around Dog, and the other around Lysandra. Together they made their way to the open windows and walked out onto the balcony. It was a glorious day of blue sky and blazing sun. Beneath the balcony several hundred townsfolk had gathered. When they saw him they cheered, and he waved at them.

"Hurrah for the Giant-Killer!" a fat woman bellowed.

A tall youth cupped his hands to his mouth and shouted, "Gods bless the Witchbane!"

Sir Edric looked suspiciously at Dog, who had the good sense to avert his eyes.

Giant-Killer? Witchbane?

"Dog… what on earth have you been doing? You were meant to make all haste in your quest to Mount Nevermore. I could have died!"

Dog coughed. "Yes, sir. I'm afraid that a small coven of witches had infested the lower slopes of the mountain and attacked when I approached. On the way back I happened upon a giant that was threatening the town and, well…"

Well, perhaps just this once I shall overlook his presumptuous escapades.

***

The plan had failed, and come within a whisker of presenting a rather permanent reason why he could not attend to the King's dangerous mission. Lysandra was willing to grant only a single night of recuperation, and the puritanical mage had forbidden any sort of relaxation with lovely ladies.

Probably just as well, given recent agonies. Still, I would like to test myself and ensure everything's in working order.

Instead he was indulging himself with flesh of a different kind, namely a mighty supper of assorted meats, washed down with a variety of wines. Despite his annoyance at Dog's gallivanting and glory-hunting he had invited his manservant to dine with him, for he had come to a decision.

"It may be best if we simply drop this apothecary plan, Dog. It almost killed me today, and last time it led us to that necromantic lunatic Greymond."

Dog sipped his wine. "When the medicine is more deadly than the disease, it's perhaps time to suffer the latter rather than the former, sir."

It comes to something when the safe course of action means traipsing across hundreds of miles towards near certain doom.

The Tower of Uz-Talrak

"Your money or your life!" a weaselly-voiced highwayman demanded.

Sir Edric sighed, and continued pissing up against the tree.

"Hey, I said-"

"I heard what you said, you bloody idiot. I can hardly throw you my purse whilst I'm having a piss, can I? Just wait a bloody minute."

The thief, a stubble-faced stumpy little fellow, thought about that and nodded. "Be sure you do, or I'll gut you like a fish," he said, waving his dagger around in an attempt to be threatening.

Such is life. Only a week or two ago when I got interrupted in the middle of the night it was by a randy minx demanding satisfaction.

The substantial quantity of wine he had drunk before leaving his home earlier that day took some time to pass, so much so that the thief had sat on the ground and was drumming a beat on his knees. Once the knight had finished watering the tree the thief leapt to his feet and pointed the dagger at him.

"Your money or your life!" he demanded again.

Sir Edric rolled his eyes and unlaced the purse from his belt. He tossed it over to the thief, who felt its pleasing weight and grinned.

The knight picked up his crossbow, which had been propped up by the tree trunk, and pointed it at the thief.

"Your money or your life, peasant," Sir Edric said.

He bound the dimwit to the tree, and returned to the campfire with his purse rather heavier than before.

***

Before leaving his manor Sir Edric had taken the opportunity to peruse the library for anything that might prove enlightening. There were several tomes with snippets relating to the Unholy

Temple but, alas, all were of limited help. Timothy Gambeson's Chronicles of Misfortune and Woe was filled with stories of men who had entered the Temple and suffered terrible and fatal injuries within its walls. One poor soul had been turned inside out, or so the book claimed. The History of Magic and Mysticism, by Clarence Farwood, had offered some vague ruminations on the Unholy Temple's supposed founding but little of practical use. The Forbidden Book of Jeremy Silveroak had proven the least helpful, as the damned thing burst into flames the moment it was opened.

Thankfully, Lysandra had managed to shut the book, which extinguished the fire. She had also healed his burnt hands.

"Surely *someone* must have survived the Unholy Temple," Sir Edric remarked as they trotted northward, on the road to the Kingdom of Nurkabr.

"Nobody," the elf replied. "Oh, don't look so glum. You could be the first!"

"Second," Dog interrupted.

Sir Edric and Lysandra looked at him.

"The thief wanting to meet there must have found a safe way in and out," the manservant explained.

That's true. If some vile miscreant can navigate the Temple without lethal consequences then a man of knightly virtue should be able to do likewise.

They travelled along the road until they came by a tree upon which a parchment notice had been nailed. Sir Edric dismounted and wandered over to inspect it.

"What does it say?" Lysandra asked.

He remounted Temper. "It just informs us that the border crossing into Nurkabr is six miles distant," he said.

"The last milestone we passed said it was three," the irritatingly observant elf replied.

Why do women have to remember every bloody little thing?

She dismounted, examined the parchment herself and declared, "We must help!"

41

Of course we must.

Dog cleared his throat and his master started to explain.

"The notice says that some silly wench-" Sir Edric began.

"Princess Maria," Lysandra interjected.

"Ran off with her uncle-"

"Was brutally kidnapped."

"And is now living in a grand old house with him."

"And is being held captive in a tower, where the uncle, Prince Kuzma, intends to auction her off to the highest bidder!"

Sir Edric sighed. "So she's guaranteed a rich husband. Lucky her."

Lysandra climbed onto Hamilton's Trousers and pointed her perfectly slender finger at him. "We must save her. Women are not pieces of meat, Sir Edric."

Obviously. Pieces of meat don't talk all the bloody time.

"Have you ever been to one of those auctions?" he asked.

She shook her head. "Have you?" she asked, eyes narrowing.

"Of course not," he lied. "But I heard tales of them from Ursk prisoners during the war. It'll be crammed with the lowest, most depraved, immoral men imaginable. Powerful sorcerers, master traders, and Ursk warlords will all be there. Perhaps even a banker or two. The parchment says that Kuzma has an army of golems protecting the tower, and Uz-Talrak is five miles into Ursk territory."

Lysandra frowned. "We cannot just ride past, Sir Edric. If we cannot attack directly, what do you suggest?"

***

"I am *not* wearing this!" she insisted.

He clenched his jaw to stop the deserved grin from showing. Their best hope, he had decided, was to approach the tower as though they were bidders. Once there, they could assess the situation and try to quietly and subtly break Princess Careless out.

Unfortunately, Lysandra's pointy-ears were a problem. Elven lands were distant and they rarely travelled, and there was only one elven sorceress in the kingdom. Besides, it would be most unusual for one woman to bid for another.

Although that is a rather splendid thought.

Sir Edric himself would have little problem pretending to be a bidder. Indeed, it reminded him of old times with Orff. Dog could scarcely have been more manservantish if he had 'manservant' tattooed across his forehead. Which left the question of how to disguise Lysandra. He had wanted to simply leave her in Northtown, the tediously named northern town they had come to a mile down the road. However, she insisted upon accompanying him on the feeble claim that he might try running away if she couldn't keep her beady eye on him.

She could not claim to be his wife, and she didn't have the bearing or humility to be a servant. A concubine, on the other hand, fit perfectly...

"It's more modest than average," he protested. "Half of them go topless."

The other half are entirely naked.

The garment was of Ursk design, and made for their prettier slaves. The Ursk themselves had little interest in human women, except as hors d'oeuvres, but knew that their buyers did and so had created revealing clothing to stimulate the prices. Her right leg was covered down to the knee, and the left only half that distance. Sadly her breasts remained entirely hidden from view, but her arms and midriff were exposed. Bandages offered scant protection for her feet and covered most of her calves.

"Look, you're the one who insists on this and on coming along. If you cover up much more nobody's going to believe us."

I wonder what price I'd get for her...

She sighed and looked at Dog, who had his back to the elf and was staring at the ground for good measure.

"What do you think, Dog?" she asked.

The manservant turned around, glanced at her, and then turned back. "You look perfect, my lady. I am afraid that if we are to infiltrate Uz-Talrak that is the sort of thing that must be worn."

Reluctantly, the sorceress acquiesced and the three of them rode towards the Ursk border. No boundary stones or flags marked the end to the realm of men, but the tower, and the golems milling around it, reassured them that they were on the right path.

They took their steeds to the stables and then walked up to the wide moat that ringed the tower of Uz-Talrak. A pair of golems, each twice the height of a man, guarded the drawbridge. They were speaking to one another in rumbly voices when Sir Edric and his companions approached.

"Good day," the knight greeted them.

"Bugger off, meatsack."

"I'm here for the auction," he protested.

The first golem looked him up and down. "Nobody would want to buy you. Now get stuffed, or I'll hit you until your crunchy bits snap."

"Look, pebblebrain, I'm not here to bloody sell myself! I'm here to bid for the princess."

The twelve foot golem took a step towards him, and made a disturbing rumbling noise.

Perhaps calling him pebblebrain was unwise...

Dog unsheathed his sword and strode to Sir Edric's side.

"What's going on here?" an Ursk growled.

The two golems took a step back and turned to face the Ursk. He was halfway between their height and Sir Edric's and clad in leather armour. His frown turned upside down when he saw the knight.

At least, I hope that's a smile. Maybe he's hungry.

"Surprised to see you here, Edric," Grog Bel-Rot said.

Uh oh. I hope he's not in a bad mood...

"You know the fleshface?" one of the golems asked.

"Aye, rockhead," Grog confirmed, avoiding eye contact with Dog and staring at the scantily clad elf. The Ursk strolled down the drawbridge and pointed at the sorceress with a massive clawed hand. "Who's the pointy-ear?"

Sir Edric slapped Lysandra on the posterior and put a possessive arm around her shoulders. "This rampant elven totty is Freya." He smiled at the elf, who did not reciprocate. "A man needs a bed-warmer, after all. There's no problem if I attend the auction, is there?"

"No problem at all. Bidding starts tomorrow. And Edric?"

"Yes?"

Grog smiled at Lysandra. "Let me know if you want to sell the elf."

***

Sir Edric gurgled, but his most strenuous efforts were insufficient to break free of the enraged creature that had pinned him to the wall and was slowly choking the life from him.

I knew I shouldn't have smacked her. Woe is me, seduced by the forbidden promise of a delightful elven derrière!

"If you ever try spanking me again you won't have to wait for the Unholy Temple to end up dead!" Lysandra hissed.

They were in his surprisingly spacious quarters on the fourth floor, and she was taking the opportunity to register her discontent with his behaviour earlier in the day. Dog had been dispatched to fetch some wine, leaving the two alone.

Suddenly her magical grip on him disappeared and he crashed heavily onto the stone floor. Lysandra slumped into a chair and Sir Edric staggered to his feet.

"As you wish, but I can hardly pretend not to… enjoy your company. You are pretending to be my concubine, you know," he said, easing his bruised body into the chair beside her.

She gave him a distinctly unimpressed look.

"I think it would be best if you spent the night here." The sorceress rose to her feet and he held his hands up to placate her. "No, no, not like that. Well, not unless you want to. I simply meant that the servants' quarters will likely be a collection of tightly packed bunks. Being my concubine, nobody will be surprised if you spend the night in these rather comfortable quarters. It's that, or spend the night with scores of grubby servants."

Lysandra nodded. "Very well. It is a gracious gesture for you to let me have your bed. I trust the floor will not be too uncomfortable for you?"

Sir Edric winked at her. "Grog told me there's a feast being held this evening. I shall attend, as will Dog. Tonight we'll learn what we can and try to discover where the princess is being kept. If we can find a way to break her out, tonight would be the best time, so don't sleep too heavily."

* * *

There were rather more guests at the feast than Sir Edric had expected. He recognised Prince Kuzma. The two men had met two decades ago during the victory celebrations after the Battle of Hornska had forced the Ursk to negotiate a peace treaty. Time had not been kind to the younger brother of King Boris. His belly was fat as a hippopotamus and a second chin wobbled beneath his first. Worst of all was his hair. Most of it had fallen out, and instead of shaving the rest or cutting it short he had grown it long and combed it over.

His head of hair is about as convincing as a beardless dwarf.

There was also Grog Bel-Rot, who smiled a rather unnerving hello at Sir Edric. The knight did not know him nearly so well as Orff No-Balsac, but he was uncomfortably familiar with Grog's murderous reputation.

He knew few of the others, and found himself seated between a pair of strangers. A sorcerer was on his left and a hideously flatulent merchant was to his right.

"And who might you be?" the sorcerer demanded. Sir Edric knew he was a sorcerer, partly because he wore the ornate robes of the Order of the Seven Truths, and partly because he was a supercilious git.

He made a point of finishing his cup of wine before replying. "Sir Edric Greenlock, Hero of Hornska. And you're some wand-fondler or other."

Sir Edric held up his cup and Dog stepped forward to fill it before taking a few paces backwards. Every man present had a single servant to refill their cups. Behind the mage was a well-built man who had the look of a bodyguard.

"I am Cyrus the Magnificent!" the sorcerer proclaimed grandly.

"Never heard of you."

"I would not expect some dull-witted knight, good for nothing but primitive labour, to be familiar with those of us endowed with superior intellects and the immense power of the Seven Truths," Cyrus the Self-Regarding replied.

The merchant broke wind loudly, and, red-faced, apologised.

I'm surrounded by men talking out of their backsides.

One of the serving girls offered a platter of meat.

"What is it?" Sir Edric asked. Whilst he loved meat, bitter experience had taught him that the Ursk tended to prefer cheaper stuff, such as horse or human. The girl claimed it was beef, but he decided to err on the side of caution and waved it away.

"Primitive labour?" Sir Edric laughed. "I don't recall seeing many sorcerers in war. Frightened of battle? Scared of the Ursk? We wouldn't want you to soil your pretty robes, would we?"

Cyrus scowled. "The risks we face manipulating the arcane and travelling the netherworld are far more terrible than any battle fought with mundane means."

Sir Edric shrugged. "Oh, indeed. One sorcerer I knew suffered a horrific paper cut from all that reading."

He held up his cup, and when Dog drew near he muttered, "I need a distraction to leave unnoticed. Go find an Ursk and challenge him to a wrestling match."

Dog sighed. "Indeed, sir."

Oh, don't look so glum. It's hardly the first time. And what's the worst that could happen? Well, death, I suppose, but that's unlikely.

"Wait for me in my quarters with Lysandra," the knight added.

An approving roar signalled that Dog's challenge had been accepted, and all the Ursk present, including two that had been guarding the staircase to the sixth floor, ran forward to watch. Many of the men and Fyntok present did likewise, but the sorcerer, far above such vulgar entertainment, remained in his seat. When Sir Edric got up and began walking towards the stairs the sorcerer asked him what he was doing.

"Have you finished with this bottle?" Sir Edric enquired, pointing at an empty vessel.

The sorcerer nodded, and Sir Edric smashed it over the back of his head, knocking him out. The sound could not be heard over the raucous cheering of the Ursk watching the wrestling, although the sorcerer's bodyguard saw what happened.

Bugger, I forgot about his servant.

"Arrogant prick," the servant muttered. "I wish I'd got to do that."

Sir Edric strolled off before anyone else saw him.

He crept surreptitiously up the spiral staircase. Above the fifth floor, where the feast was still being held, was Princess Maria's bedchamber. He had no idea whether there would be more guards higher up and moved as cautiously as he could, dagger at the ready.

Fortune smiled upon him, for there were none on the sixth floor. He sheathed his dagger and strolled over to the nearest door. Placing his eye to the keyhole he peered in and saw it was just a storage room piled high with barrels, sacks and boxes. The next door, however, yielded the sight he was looking for.

I can hear the coins clinking already. If she's worth her weight in gold then I'm going to be very rich.

Princess Maria, tall, blonde and built like a brick privy, was going through the motions of some sort of martial art. Somewhat surprisingly she was fully dressed, despite the late hour, and wearing trousers.

I should get back to the feast before I'm missed. Grog's not the sort to let friendship get in the way of brutally murdering someone.

He got up, wandered over to a window made up of scores of little lead-lined panes and peered outside. A blazing tripod by the entrance illuminated the two rockheads guarding the drawbridge, but there did not seem to be any more golems between the tower and the stables.

"Hey!" a voice startled him. Sir Edric turned around and saw an axe-wielding Ursk striding towards him. "What the hell are you doing? The bidders aren't allowed on this floor, and we've orders to make an example of anyone we find. Give up your weapons."

Sir Edric did so, unbuckling and tossing away his belt, which held his sword and dagger. He held his hands up in surrender. "I'm sorry, but I heard a strange noise. And just look outside. I think someone's trying to mount a rescue."

He stood to one side as the hulking Ursk approached the window and looked outside. "I can't see anyone attempting a rescue."

Sir Edric kicked the Ursk's broad backside with all his might and sent the lofty creature stumbling forwards. It crashed through the window and plummeted through the air, splashing into the moat far below.

Should've looked behind you.

He hurriedly buckled on his belt, but saw that the Ursk had actually survived the fall and was swimming towards land.

Damn. No, wait a second, that's perfect. If I can jump and live all I need do is retrieve my horses and flee. Huzzah!

He prepared himself for the immense drop, but just managed to stop himself from jumping. Something in the moat had dragged the screaming Ursk to a watery death, and it looked like blood was rising to the surface.

Bugger.

Moving with great haste he hurried down the stairs and found the feast had finished. A pair of Ursk still guarded the staircase and frowned at him as he appeared.

"What're you doing?" one of them asked him. "Nobody's supposed to be above the fifth floor. We've got orders to stop anyone going up."

Sir Edric frowned. "I'm not above the fifth floor, and I'm going down, not up."

The Ursk's minuscule brain was dumbfounded by the unexpected answer and the knight walked off before either guard could stop him.

Lysandra was, as expected, in his quarters, and so was Dog. The pair were seated at the table with an empty bottle of wine for company.

"You're later than we expected. Been busy ogling the princess, have we?"

Sir Edric sighed. "After a little searching I managed to find her. An Ursk guard spotted me and we fought. Thankfully he was no match for my swordplay, and I threw him out of a sixth floor window to teach him a lesson."

"So, can we save Princess Maria?" Lysandra asked.

"Getting to her and breaking her out of her room should not be too difficult, but there are hundreds of guests and Ursk and golems between the sixth floor and safety… unless…" A deliciously brilliant idea was beginning to form in his mind, and he grinned. "Dog, take some coin and go speak to one of the slavers. We've got a small purchase to make."

***

Harriet had been surprised to be bought, and astounded when, moments later, Sir Edric had given her some new clothes and freed her on condition she went to Northtown right away. Lysandra had been confused by his generous act, until she realised what his purpose was.

"You're just a drooling pervert, aren't you?"

He scowled. "I am not *just* a drooling pervert. Hero of Hornska, slayer of Ursk, freer of slaves, rescuer of damsels in distress." He sighed. "Seducer of queens. Well, one queen."

Lysandra smirked. "And how did that work out for you?"

Very well, until her husband found out.

Harriet's former slave raiment, which consisted of very short shorts matching those Lysandra wore, would be taken for Princess Maria to wear. Sir Edric would then be able to simply walk out with his 'slave' and they'd be away before the sun rose. Only the two Ursk guarding the staircase would prove an obstacle, and an easy one at that.

Lysandra unwound the bandage that protected her right calf and handed it to Sir Edric. "A princess cannot wander around topless," she haughtily informed him.

Really? Her Royal Hotness rather enjoyed prancing around without the burden of clothing.

"Better hand me the other bandage too," he suggested. "She's built like an Ursk."

Sir Edric and Dog took the lead with Lysandra hanging back, ready to intervene if anything went wrong. The feasting hall was utterly abandoned, save for the two Ursk who were sat at one table gnawing on meat of a dubious nature.

"Fancy a game of cards?" Sir Edric suggested, brandishing a deck at the brutes.

The nearer Ursk broke wind and spat a bone in the knight's direction. "You ain't meant to be here."

Dog, who had subtly worked his way behind the pair whilst his master distracted them, smacked a chair over the back of the first Ursk's head. The second had time to get to his feet and turn before Dog introduced his knee to the creature's groin and knocked him out with an uppercut.

"Ow," the manservant complained, shaking his hand. "I'd forgotten just how hard their jaws are."

Lysandra crept into the chamber and smiled at Dog. "Well done."

"Thank you," Sir Edric replied. "And stop being such a girl, Dog. It's better than killing them. You know what Grog's like. With them alive he'll take his anger out on them for failing, rather than trying to chase us down. Well, hopefully. Both of you stay here and guard the staircase."

"Won't you need help breaking through the door?" Lysandra asked.

He flexed both biceps, although she did not look very impressed.

All that reading's probably damaged her eyesight.

"You underestimate my might. Magic's not the only thing that can get through doors. Now, you wait here. I shan't be long."

He ran up the stairs, acutely aware of the need for speed, and bumped into the massive Ursk standing at the top waiting for him.

"Good evening, Edric," Grog greeted him. "Going for a walk?"

His hulking body blocked the way to the princess' chamber, but the ugly lump of bone that served as his mace was still in his belt. Grog gestured at the gaping hole where the window had once been. Jagged glass teeth ringed the hole and shards that glittered in the moonlight were strewn across the floor.

"You should be careful walking around the tower at night. It seems Lug Ur-Arz accidentally wandered through a window," he remarked. Grog picked a lump of gristly meat from between his teeth with a claw. "Poor sod. Survived the landing, thanks to the moat, but then got dragged to a gruesome fate by the water dragon." He smiled at Sir Edric.

Uh oh...

"You're trying to rescue the princess, aren't you?"

"It's strictly for the money," Sir Edric confessed. Unlike most Ursk, Grog was no fool and lying would get him nowhere.

Grog punched him in the stomach and he collapsed to his knees. The Ursk's huge hand grasped the top of his skull and held him in the air.

"Anything you'd like to say before I throw you out of the window?"

"Wait! I can get you money. Wagons of gold!"

Grog strolled over to the glassless window and held Sir Edric outside, his feet dangling above thin air.

"Do continue."

"I'm going to the Unholy Temple on a mission for the King, but in case I fail he's sending a ransom along the same route. If you wait before Northtown you'll be able to ambush it," Sir Edric gabbled. He looked down at the distant moat and closed his eyes.

Don't let go. Please don't let go.

He felt movement, and opened his eyes. Grog dropped him back inside the tower.

"How much, and when?"

"One hundred thousand solidi, probably in a week or two."

Grog's eyes widened, and he slapped Sir Edric. It felt like being struck with an anvil.

"Are you taking the piss, Edric? A hundred thousand solidi? You could buy yourself a kingdom for that."

"Cross my heart and hope to be thrown from a sixth floor window."

The Ursk stroked his jutting chin for a moment. "Why didn't you just make this deal when you saw me?"

I... actually that would've been rather more sensible.

"You'll be gone by morning?" the Ursk asked, handing Sir Edric a key, presumably to the princess' chamber.

The knight nodded. "You'll stop anyone pursuing?"

Grog shrugged. "I'll eat Kuzma and a few others. The rest'll be no bother. I'll see you again, Edric." He turned to walk away, and then turned back, "And if there are no wagons of gold I'll hunt you down and sell you to Ganska."

Sir Edric shuddered.

Hopefully I'll be dead by then.

Hurrying, he ran to the warrior princess' bedchamber and unlocked it. She was asleep, but awoke with a start when she saw him.

"Shh! Put these on and then come with me," he ordered her, tossing the minuscule garments to the princess.

Princess Maria threw the tiny clothes on the floor and spat in his face. "I'm not your harlot, you slaver bastard. Come near me and I'll gouge your bloody eyes out."

Her gratitude is matched only by her beauty.

"I'm here to rescue you, you silly bitch," he retorted. "Just put those on and we'll walk out of the tower, then you can put on some proper clothes again."

Princess Maria looked dumbfounded and then picked up the clothes. "Alright. Thank you. Oh, there is something you need to know."

"What?"

She punched him in the face and he staggered backwards.

"Nobody calls me a silly bitch. If you weren't helping me I'd break your legs, you cocky bastard. Now get outside while I get changed."

Maybe she's Grog's bastard daughter.

54

The door slammed shut behind him. Moments later the princess emerged. Her muscular frame coupled with the skimpy outfit made her appear more like a gladiator than a concubine.

Is it my imagination, or is she splitting the shorts?

Maria saw him staring and he stepped back, hands raised in surrender. "Come with me. My companions are waiting for us."

He led her swiftly down the stairs to where Lysandra and Dog were waiting.

"This is Dog, my faithful manservant, and this is Lysandra, a powerful sorceress."

Powerful, and pretentious.

Sir Edric informed them that Grog had agreed to prevent any pursuit, but did not deign to mention the information that had bought the Ursk's co-operation. The knight led the manservant, sorceress and princess as quickly as he could without arousing suspicion down the tower and then out onto the drawbridge.

"What're you doing here, meatsack? Don't your kind sleep at night?" one of the golems carped at Sir Edric.

Lysandra raised her hands and from each one a spike of ice flew. The two golems were transfixed, and from the projectiles a thin but rapidly thickening layer of ice spread across them. Within a moment they were encased in icy prisons.

The four ran for the stables. Sir Edric offered to help Princess Beefcake onto Hamilton's Trousers but the haughty maiden sneered at his hand and practically leapt onto the poor horse.

If you make my horse lame I'll give you a thrashing, woman or no.

The princess did not wait for them and galloped away. Sir Edric was about to offer Lysandra the opportunity to ride Temper with him, but the irksome elf had already climbed onto Twenty-Six. Her arms were wrapped tightly around Dog.

Lucky swine. Still, onwards to glory and gold!

An Unwanted Gift

Nurkagorod, capital of Nurkabr, was several days riding to the north. Princess Maria had despaired of travelling with them, bought herself a horse in Northtown and galloped off to return to her father alone.

Just as well. Bloody woman was riding Hamilton's Trousers into the ground.

The three of them had reached a bridge over a wide river and he glanced across at the horse Lysandra was riding. She had changed back into her usual garb, though he noticed she hadn't thrown away the slave clothes. Hamilton's Trousers appeared a little worse for wear, though his gait was fine.

It's a shame we aren't walking. I could push her into the river and by the time she swam free I'd be long gone.

They camped by the wayside for the night and, before the sun set, Sir Edric and Dog engaged in a little sparring. The quarterstaff was the weapon of choice and the two men, elated with the success of the rescue, went at it hammer and tongs. They fought at a blistering pace and a stranger would imagine the men were trying to kill one another. Suddenly, Sir Edric swept Dog's legs from under him and planted the quarterstaff against his throat.

"Huzzah! Well fought, Dog," he said, holding out a hand to help his manservant up.

When was the last time I beat him? Probably three years ago... although he was quite drunk at the time.

Dog smiled and bowed his head. "Thank you, sir. Should I get started on supper?"

Sir Edric looked around and was surprised to see that it was almost night, and that a certain elf had been watching. "Yes, and help yourself to filseed oil if you need it."

I did give you quite the drubbing, after all.

"Enjoy yourself?" Lysandra asked him.

The knight wiped some of the sweat from his forehead and grinned. "Yes, actually. Yesterday I saved a princess from a tower and I imagine King Boris will give me an immense reward."

"Given you think you're a dead man walking I'm surprised you care about gold."

Sir Edric shrugged. "We're all dead men walking, it's just a question of when we stop. Whilst I'm still strolling around I'd rather do so with a fat purse than a thin one."

The two of them wandered to the campsite and enjoyed a little pottage for supper. Whilst they were eating, a question that had been burrowing its way through Sir Edric's brain finally reached his tongue.

"So, why are mages forbidden from entering the Unholy Temple?"

She sighed. "In the ancient times it was used to sacrifice those whom men considered witches, namely anyone with any magical talent at all. Diabolical runes are carved into the walls and prevent any magic being done within the foul temple."

The knight nodded. "Are the runes magic?"

"Yes."

He frowned. "But isn't that paradoxical? If the runes stop magic working, surely they'd stop their own magic? And if they did then magic would work. So they'd be able to stop magic. And then they wouldn't work, so then they would. It doesn't make any sense."

Lysandra swiftly finished off the last of her wine. "I am not going to try and explain complex arcane theory to someone sadly unblessed by the divine gift of magic. Goodnight, gentlemen."

***

Sir Edric was tired, and it was not the happy sort of exhaustion that filled a man after a hard-won victory on the field of battle, or in the bedroom. It was the weariness of a day too long. Lysandra, keen to make up for time lost faffing around saving Princess Maria, had forced him to rise before dawn and ride until well past nightfall. Only good fortune had enabled them to reach Sarastok, a small village in Nurkabr on the way to the capital, and enjoy the rare chance to sleep under a roof.

He had slept like the dead, an experience he imagined he would soon become very familiar with, until a knocking on his door stole him away from the comfortable arms of slumber. The knight peered up at the window and saw that it was still dark outside. The faintest golden glimmers of dawn were creeping over the horizon.

Gods, what time is it? I may not be able to evade this deadly quest but I'm damned if I'm going to be woken before dawn every bloody morning.

Sir Edric threw aside his sheets, pulled on his boots and stomped over to the door. He flung it open and prepared to give Lysandra a piece of his mind.

"I'm sorry for disturbing you," said a pretty little redhead he had seen in the tavern last night. She was wearing a thin green kirtle, the laces of which were fighting a losing battle against her ample breasts. "But I heard some men say that you were Sir Edric, the saviour of Nurkabr. Is it true?"

Gods bless young ladies and their affection for heroes.

"Yes, it is. Might I know your name?"

"Natalya," she said with a pretty little giggle. "I'm sorry for disturbing you at this hour… I've been trying to work up the courage to come and knock on your door. I was wondering if you might like some company-"

"Ah, I thought I heard something. Glad to see you're awake already," Lysandra interrupted, walking up behind the redhead. "Splendid, we must hurry on our quest. No time for dilly-dallying, or other such… distractions," she said, casting a distinctly unimpressed eye over Natalya.

"I'm sorry, I didn't realise you were with someone," Natalya said. She curtsied, and left before either Sir Edric or Lysandra could correct her.

If I wanted a life of chastity I'd live with my wife.

"Surely we can at least get something to eat first? Breakfast is the most important meal of the day."

The elf agreed, and they strolled down the creaking wooden stairs to the bar. He saw a dubious, drying stain on the floor just in time to step over it and tell Lysandra to watch her feet. The hour was early indeed, for they had little company. The barman was snoozing, and Dog had his nose buried in a book. The only others present were a prowling tabby cat and a soldier. He wore the distinctive wolf-head helm and fur armour that the army of Nurkabr favoured. Upon seeing the knight, the soldier raised his tankard in salute, and Sir Edric nodded back politely. Lysandra went to join Dog at his table, and Sir Edric took a seat at the bar. The barman was snoring quietly, face down on the bar.

Sir Edric sighed, then thumped the bar noisily. The barman awoke with a start, and looked around in confusion.

"Are the Ursk attacking?" he asked.

"No, you narcoleptic nincompoop. It's morning, or very late night, or some sort of interdiem, pre-dawn period. Anyway, I'm looking for a spot of breakfast. Some roast beef, bacon and two pints of beer, if you please."

The bartender sighed. "Terribly sorry, but the cook was stricken with the bloody flux yesterday. So, I'm afraid hot food is off the menu."

"Well, what do you have?"

The barman knelt behind the bar and furkled around for a moment, before standing back up and putting a sausage of some sort and a dark loaf of bread on the bar. Sir Edric tapped the bread hesitantly.

I've been hit by maces softer than that. Still at least the sausage looks-

59

Before his sleep-addled brain could conclude its thought, the tabby leapt upon the table, pounced upon the sausage and ran off.

-nice.

"And what fine beverages can you offer?"

"Ursk raiders stole the last beer shipment, and we ran out of what beer we had last night... but we still have plenty of water."

Marvellous.

The knight's stomach complained loudly about its neglect, and he reluctantly grasped the chunk of iron masquerading as bread. When he touched the loaf an unfamiliar insect as long as a finger bone burrowed its way out of the bread and stood on the bar, antennae twitching.

"On second thoughts I'll give breakfast a miss."

The journey north was unpleasant. Sir Edric disliked riding on an empty stomach, and the pre-dawn darkness echoed his gloomy mood. When the sun rose he spotted a small forest a mile or two from the road.

"We need something to eat. Let me see if I can catch anything in the forest," he said.

Lysandra considered, and then replied, "Very well. But be swift. We cannot afford any more delays."

Oh, yes. Mustn't be late for my appointment with highly probable death.

He left Dog and Lysandra on the road and had Temper trot towards the forest. Just as he was about to enter it a pair of shabby peasants with sacks over their shoulders emerged.

"Argh! A centaur!" the first of them yelped.

"I'm not a centaur, I'm a man on a horse," Sir Edric replied, eyeing their sacks suspiciously. "I'm Sir Edric. Who are you, and what're you doing here?"

The second man answered, "We aren't poachers."

"You are poachers, aren't you?"

The two men looked at one another. "Yes."

"I really should carry out a summary execution…" the knight mused, raising his crossbow and pulling back the bolt so that it was ready to fire.

The pair of empty-headed peasants fell to their knees. "Please, spare us! We're just simple, starving folk, desperate for a good meal."

Sir Edric pointed his crossbow at the nearer of the rustic bumpkins, who squealed in terror. "Well, perhaps I could be merciful. It is a knightly duty, after all. Very well, peasants, I hereby confiscate your ill-gotten gains on behalf of King Boris and spare your lives. But if I catch you poaching again I shall put you in a sack with an angry weasel. Now, begone!"

The unfortunate pair bowed their heads and then ran off towards the road. Sir Edric dismounted Temper and inspected the sacks, crossbow at the ready just in case. There was a delightful sufficiency of meat, mostly hare and squirrel, but with a nice helping of pigeon and a lone deer. Happy with his haul, he tied the neck of the sack to his saddle and went back to his companions.

When he returned to the road he found that Dog and Lysandra had been accosted by a score of soldiers wearing the fur armour and wolf-head helms of Nurkabr.

"Is there a problem?" he asked, raising his voice to attract the attention of the soldiers.

The men turned to face him, and greeted his arrival with a chorus of gasps and cheers. One of them, an older man with a greying moustache, approached the knight.

"We didn't believe your servants when they claimed to be travelling with the Hero of Hornska," the man said. "I must apologise, Sir Edric."

Sir Edric smiled, more at the thought of Lysandra being his servant than at the apology.

"I'm Sergeant Vladimir," the soldier continued, stepping near enough for his powerful odour to offend Sir Edric's nose. "We met briefly during the Battle of Hornska. It was an honour to fight alongside you, sir."

Did we? I'm sure a smell like that would leave an indelible stain on my memory.

"The honour was all mine," Sir Edric assured Sergeant Vladimir, slapping the man on the shoulder.

Sergeant Vladimir offered to escort them to Nurkagorod, where King Boris would once again wish to reward Sir Edric for his heroism rescuing Princess Maria, and the knight gladly accepted. Whilst he and the sergeant led the little column and chattered about how marvellous Sir Edric was Lysandra sought Dog's company.

"Please tell me this hero-worship won't happen when we reach the city," she implored the servant.

Dog coughed. "Well, it probably won't be quite as extravagant as last time, after Hornska."

Lysandra raised a plucked eyebrow. "What happened? Or don't I want to know?"

Dog smiled. "I suspect you would rather not, my lady."

***

Everywhere they went villagers, farmers and soldiers turned out to cheer and applaud Sir Edric, who beamed with delight at the attention and waved to each and every one. The ride into Nurkagorod was the happiest Sir Edric had been since his failed attempt to flee and evade the almost certainly fatal mission Lawrence had sent him on. King Boris, a tremendously fat fellow, emerged from the city's gates atop the unluckiest horse in the kingdom to greet the knight personally.

"Edric, most blessed of men!" the King bellowed, his thunderous voice echoed by a cacophony of cheers from the surrounding crowds. "Decades ago you saved my entire kingdom, and now you've rescued my delicate flower from the clutches of that wretch Kuzma."

Maria? She's about as delicate as rhino hide.

"Splendid to see you again, Boris," Sir Edric said. The King was a fine drinking partner, and a generous man. After so many unfriendly faces in recent days he was a welcome sight.

Sergeant Vladimir, escort duties complete, was dismissed by the King. Boris and Sir Edric, preceded by the monarch's royal guard, rode into Nurkagorod, followed by Lysandra and Dog. They rode in triumph into the city where hordes lined the roads and rooftops and cheered to see the return of the Hero of Hornska.

"Could I enquire as to when I might get my reward?" Sir Edric asked. "I hate to rush things, but unfortunately that milksop Lawrence has sent me on a mission and time is tighter than a whore's corset."

Boris laughed and slapped Sir Edric on the back. "Aye, the chinless wonder sent me a letter telling me so. I'll get you the gold after supper. You're more than welcome to come and stay here, regardless of what Lawrence says."

Sir Edric glanced backwards at Lysandra. "I'd love to, but I fear the prim and proper sorceress accompanying me would fry me to a crisp."

Several hundred yards into the city was a grand crossroads of wide avenues, and in its very centre was a statue of stone that soared sixty feet high. It depicted a rather younger Sir Edric, foot planted atop a decapitated Ursk. One hand clutched the beast's severed head, whilst the other held aloft his sword.

He smiled at the gargantuan stone image of himself. The statue seemed to be faring better than he was.

At least when I die there will forever be a crossroads that remembers me... as well as a certain frisky queen, of course.

***

He spent only a single night in the city, but being feted, toasted, praised and cheered did wonders for Sir Edric's mood. Ever

63

since that fateful night when his nocturnal rendezvous with Lawrence's wife had been interrupted he had veered from mortal woe to deadly peril and it made a very pleasant change to be somewhere he was not merely safe but lauded. His weapons were sharpened by the royal blacksmith, King Boris festooned him with golden gifts as a reward for rescuing his manly daughter and, as they approached the gate to leave the city, the monarch presented him with a final surprise.

"I know I can't help you avoid this terrible quest, but perhaps I can help you survive it," Boris said. There were few people lining the streets to mark Sir Edric's departure, as they were setting off as dawn approached. Here and there beautiful maidens threw roses and soldiers hefted their spears in salute, but the streets were largely deserted.

"I have someone to help you on your journey," the King revealed. "He awaits outside the gate."

I hope it's a horse. A horse or a hound. Or a magical hybrid horsehound! A magical winged horsehound. That can breathe fire.

"It's not a sorcerer, is it?" Sir Edric asked warily. Not only did magicians tend to be full of themselves, they were also unable to use their powers within the Unholy Temple.

King Boris grinned and tugged on his horse's reins to come to a stop. "Nay, Sir Edric. But one of our finest warriors. Tremendously skilful, righteous and obedient."

Sounds like an obsequious little shit to me.

The King sighed. "I must be honest, part of the reason I'm sending him with you is that he's a chirpy bugger and he's been getting on my wick, but if he helps you survive that's a price worth paying, is it not?"

This does sound suspiciously like you're foisting the most annoying man in Nurkabr on me...

The King cleared his throat and shouted, "Come forth!" through the gate.

A pure white steed upon which sat a young, handsome man dressed in leather armour trotted through the gate. He bowed his head first to the King and then to Sir Edric.

King Boris gestured at the youth. "Sir Edric, it is my pleasure to introduce Colin the Adventurer, who is to be your sworn sword on this noble quest. Colin, you of course know of Sir Edric, a renowned hero and man of outstanding merit and spotless virtue."

Sir Edric thought he heard Lysandra mutter a retort, but the Adventurer diverted his attention before he could rebuke the elf.

"Absolutely splendid to meet you, Sir Edric. With a hero of your wisdom and might to lead us we're bound to succeed!"

Maybe he isn't so bad...

"Oh, I know everybody else who has ever visited the Unholy Temple of Despair and Certain Doom has ended up being horrifically killed barely moments after stepping inside, but I'm sure we'll do better."

***

Sir Edric and Colin initially led the way north, towards the Forest of Bones, but the Adventurer refused to shut the hell up for even a moment and was giving the knight quite the headache.

At least alcohol gives me pleasure before pain. This oaf just provides tedium first.

"Anyway, I was thinking that-"

"Shut up and get to the back," Sir Edric snapped.

The brusqueness of the command bounced off of Colin's cheery face like a puppy on a trampoline, leaving his sunny disposition entirely undimmed.

"Right you are! I'll protect the rear, have no worries about that," the Adventurer promised.

Colin joined Lysandra and Dog trotted up to keep his master company at the front. Behind them Colin was already subjecting the elf to an unending verbal barrage.

"Dear gods, Dog. Does he never shut up? He's worse than a woman full of gin."

Dog smiled politely. "He's an enthusiastic young man, sir. Probably overcome with delight to be accompanying you on a quest."

"Bah," Sir Edric said, speeding up a little to extend the gap between himself and Colin. "I didn't talk all the bloody time when I was his age. I was too busy doing heroic, manly things. How old is he, anyway?"

Dog looked back, and saw that the Adventurer and sorceress were engaged in intimate conversation. "Nineteen, I believe, sir."

Sir Edric followed his manservant's gaze. Colin murmured something and Lysandra giggled girlishly.

Gods, I hope he gets leprosy of the tongue.

When the time came to stop Sir Edric took the opportunity to order the garrulous whelp to pitch the tents whilst he and Dog went hunting in some nearby woods. He didn't need Dog's help to hunt, of course, but somebody had to carry the prey back to camp. The endless chattering of Colin, and worse yet the attentiveness of Lysandra to the noisy youth, had stoked the fires of Sir Edric's heart and he took his anger out on the unfortunate creatures of the wood.

"Huzzah!" Sir Edric shouted as a bronze eagle, a large and rare bird, spiralled down to the ground after he shot it with his crossbow.

"Splendid shot, sir," Dog said.

The two men wandered back to the camp before the sun set, and found Colin playing a lute and serenading Lysandra. Upon hearing their footsteps Colin stopped strumming his instrument and waved hello.

"You've caught supper. Great! What is it?" Colin asked.

"A bronze eagle," Sir Edric announced.

Lysandra seemed less than delighted at his prize.

"How could you, Edric? Bronze eagles are beautiful and sacred creatures."

"Beautiful, sacred, and delicious," Sir Edric corrected her. She sighed at him. "Can your magic bring a bird back from the dead?"

"Such necromantic acts are forbidden," Lysandra reminded him.

"We might as well eat it then."

The eagle was, as he had predicted, delicious. Less to his taste was the amazement with which Colin met the fire Lysandra magically kindled. She seemed uncharacteristically modest when the Adventurer lavished compliments upon her.

Why does she like him so much? He's barely more than a boy. I'm a man of experience and achievements! And I know when to bloody shut up.

Sir Edric handed Colin the first watch, for he remembered that Lysandra typically lay awake reading or meditating until the second watch, when she briefly slept. Unfortunately that meant putting up with listening to the youth's incessant chattering and the entirely undeserved amusement and interest the sorceress showed in him. After a few hours Colin woke Dog, and the servant took over the watch.

Sir Edric also rose from his tent, and smiled at his manservant.

"Is he asleep already?" he asked, pointing at Colin's tent. It was a garish mixture of orange and green stripes, unlike the drab but serviceable brown tents Sir Edric had brought.

Dog nodded. "He fell asleep almost at once, I believe, sir."

The irksome creature's lute remained beside the campfire, and Sir Edric's eyes lit up at the sight of the instrument.

"Damned cold night, isn't it, Dog?"

"Yes, sir."

The knight tossed the lute onto the fire and smiled as the greedy flames consumed the wooden object. "The cockles of my heart are thoroughly warmed. Goodnight, Dog."

"Goodnight, sir."

Heroism and Horses

Sir Edric had never been so far north. Few men had, for beyond the boundaries of Nurkabr lay the fearsome Forest of Bones. The last known town inhabited by men was on the other side of the forest, and only the most ancient texts contained details of what lay past that. Soon mortal peril would be an ever-present companion for the knight. Death would stalk his every step, and surviving another day would become a feat of heroism in itself.

"I've never been this far north. Who knows what abandoned ruins, ancient tombs and mystical wonders we will encounter!" Colin said. "Isn't this exciting?"

Very exciting. Not unlike having a scorpion dropped into your trousers.

"In fact," the Adventurer continued, "I think I'll strum a tune on my lute."

Sir Edric bit the inside of his cheek to keep his face straight as the youth rummaged through the panniers his horse carried.

"I seem to have left it behind where we camped last night," Colin said, sighing sadly.

"Oh dear," Lysandra said. "I did so love to hear you play it."

"Gosh, how awful," Sir Edric added.

Dog sighed.

Colin perked up and a grin enlivened his rosy face. "Not to worry! I'll just play my flute instead." He pulled from a pannier a shining silver flute, raised it to his lips and began to play a cheery tune.

Maybe he's a demon Esmerelda sent to torture me.

***

They reached the Forest of Bones before night fell. Its green canopy stretched as far as the eye could see, and the only road into it was little more than a dirt track.

"The Forest of Bones... this must be a place of deadly danger and gruesome death. We'd better be careful!" Colin the Adventurer said.

"Actually, the Forest of Bones is thought to be uninhabited, and is named after Theodore Bones, the famous cartographer," Sir Edric corrected the excitable youth.

Lysandra raised a plucked eyebrow in surprise at his knowledge.

"Before Hornska the forest was scouted to ensure the Ursk hadn't hidden troops there," he explained.

Sir Edric clicked his tongue and Temper resumed a trot towards the forest. There was not even the vaguest air of menace inside. It was pleasant and green, sparrows twittered, squirrels scampered and wood pigeons screeched in fright when Sir Edric shot one of their number.

They came upon a small clearing and decided to make camp. To avoid Colin's endless enthusiasm Sir Edric and Dog wandered off to hunt. The forest was teeming with deer, badgers, and rabbits, presumably because nobody lived nearby to thin their numbers.

"A successful hunt once again, Dog," Sir Edric remarked as his manservant put a brace of rabbits into his sack, where they joined a full-grown deer. "Isn't it splendid?"

"Indeed, sir," Dog agreed, groaning as he hefted the weighty sack over his shoulder.

On the way back to the camp Sir Edric swigged from his wineskin and whistled a jaunty tune, until an unexpected sight silenced him.

The overgrown, ruined remnants of a small stone outpost squatted in the forest like a mouldy loaf of bread in an abandoned kitchen. A tower had tumbled, leaving behind a fifteen foot stone husk. The walls were largely intact but utterly covered by greenery.

"What do you make of that, Dog?" Sir Edric asked, pointing his crossbow at the ruin.

"It appears to be a ruin, sir," Dog replied.

If I wanted someone with the power to state the obvious I would've gone hunting with Colin.

"Hard to see through the fecund foliage but I'd hazard a guess that's Late Seleucid architecture. Rather a surprise, actually. Most scholars believe the Seleucid Empire never got this far," Dog continued.

That's more like it.

"Seleucids, eh…" Sir Edric said, casting his mind back to the dim and distant memory of his school days and the important lessons he had learnt as a youth.

Always sit to the left of ladies. You can see through the buttons of their shirts and enjoy a splendid view.

He frowned and dragged his mind away from such titillating thoughts towards the gloomier realm of scholarship.

The Seleucids were fond of magic, golems, runes, glyphs and so forth. This place could be a festering deathtrap of arcane woe.

"Fascinating as the mossy rocks are, we had best return to camp."

Dog raised an eyebrow. "Are you sure, sir? The Late Seleucids did have a habit of decorating their architecture with ornamental gemstones."

Sir Edric assigned the important duty of guarding the sack of meat to himself, and had Dog poke around in the ruin for traps. When no blazing fireball immolated the servant, Sir Edric strolled into the outpost and handed the weighty sack back to Dog.

"So, whereabouts would they keep these precious jewels?" he asked.

"The walls and statues, sir."

The knight began the business of cutting away the thick, furry moss and enormous leaves that covered the walls and soon found several empty niches that appeared to have once held such treasures.

"Huzzah!" he cried in triumph when he came across a sapphire an inch wide embedded in a wall. After prising it free he redoubled his efforts but found nothing else on the walls.

In the middle of what had once been the outpost's courtyard was a lone pillar perhaps seven feet in height. Sir Edric cut free the greenery that had been obscuring it, and discovered that it was no pillar but a crudely carved statue. Two glinting diamonds as large as his thumbnail occupied its eye sockets. He jammed his dagger underneath the first and started to force it loose.

"Cease and desist, foul thief, or I shall crush you," the statue, which turned out to be a golem, said.

Sir Edric was so startled he yelped in surprise and dropped his dagger. After retrieving it he apologised to the golem. "Terribly sorry, old bean. I thought you were just a lump of stone."

The golem sighed. "You bloody racist! And a thief, to boot. What a despicable trespasser you are. Return that jewel," it said, pointing at the sapphire the knight still held. "It is the property of the Seleucid Empire."

Sir Edric looked around the overgrown ruin. "The Seleucid Empire fell a thousand years ago."

"Irrelevant."

Sir Edric raised an eyebrow. "Very relevant. To whom does it belong? You?"

"The Emperor."

He sighed. "The Emperor's dead, I'm afraid, and has been for centuries."

"Actually, sir," Dog intervened, "Emperor Kazimir went missing, although-"

"Shut up, Dog. The point is, the Emperor hasn't been seen for a thousand years, and the empire has crumbled into dust. It has no sorcerers, princes, soldiers, citizens, merchants or scruffy peasants. It is an ex-empire, it has ceased to be."

"It's the principle of the thing," the golem insisted. "Return the sapphire at once."

A suspicion blossomed in Sir Edric's mind, and he held out the jewel. "Certainly. Just take a few steps and reclaim it."

Over the centuries the golem had not only become entangled in countless plants but had also sunk several feet into the earth. The stone guardian grunted and groaned but was utterly unable to move.

So much for the Seleucid Empire's might. I wonder if one day I'll end up so feeble... It seems unlikely, given my highly probable death in the next few days.

"I appear to be stuck," the golem confessed. "Would you mind cutting me free?"

"Yes, actually. Goodbye," Sir Edric replied before walking away at a rather brisk pace.

It soon transpired that his insouciance was ill-judged, for barely had he left the decaying remnants of the outpost than a monstrous crumbling sound came from within. Without wasting the time to look back he broke into a run, Dog at his heels. Behind them the sound of the lumbering golem smashing its way through the forest drew ever nearer. Sir Edric risked a glance behind, and was distressed to see that the golem was within a hundred yards. He was already tired, but tried to run faster. Alas, fate was not kind because the trees abruptly ended at a sheer cliff overlooking a small lake.

"Any cunning plans, Dog?" Sir Edric asked.

"I imagine the golem is impervious to our weapons, sir," the manservant unhelpfully replied. "We could try reasoning with it."

Worth a try, although given I tried to gouge its eye out when we first met I'm not sure it'll go well.

In the moments before the golem arrived Sir Edric tried to get his breath back and affect an air of calm. The golem burst through the trees, and advanced menacingly.

"Good day," Sir Edric greeted the rockhead jovially.

"Foul thief. Return the sapphire to me at once!"

The golem, which appeared rather taller than Sir Edric recalled, took a giant step forward. The knight took a smaller step back and his heart leapt into his mouth when his foot caused several pebbles to tumble down the cliff. He looked over the edge.

Gods, that's a long way.

The golem opened its massive stone hand and held it out. "The sapphire. Now."

"And then you'll let me go?"

"And then I shall give you a mercifully swift death."

That's about as tempting an offer as a threesome with a leper and a corpse.

Sir Edric sighed with resignation at his fate. "So be it. If the sapphire is truly your desire, then go and get it!" he said, flinging the precious stone over the edge of the cliff.

The golem clumped forward, long arm and huge hand outstretched to seize its prize. To Sir Edric's dismay the metamorphic man actually caught the sapphire and managed to slow down enough to stop itself from falling over the edge of the cliff. The golem turned around to face Sir Edric.

"Now I have the sapphire, thief. And you shall have a slow, agonising death."

There was a disturbing rumbling noise from the golem, and then Sir Edric realised it came not from the pebblebrain's mouth, but its feet. The cliff edge gave way beneath the golem's immense weight, and the stone soldier, sapphire still gripped tightly in its hand, plunged hundreds of feet through the air.

Sir Edric and Dog scrambled backwards in case any more of the cliff fell away, and the knight sighed with relief at his unexpected survival.

He returned to the camp without further incident, and was dismayed to see that although the tents had been pitched and some firewood gathered the elf and the youth were nowhere to be seen.

Where could they... oh, gods. That's just not fair. That filthy fornicating pair!

"Set the sack down, Dog. We may as well enjoy the meal ourselves. It looks as though our lusty companions have found themselves something else upon which to feast."

Something else was wrong, and Sir Edric suddenly realised what it was.

"Where the bloody hell are the horses?" he exclaimed, leaping to his feet.

Temper, Twenty-Six, Hamilton's Trousers and Colin's steed, who was altogether more agreeable than her rider, were all missing. Even if Lysandra and Colin had run off to frolic in the forest they would not have taken every horse.

"They must have been captured," Dog reasoned.

"We must rescue them!" Sir Edric declared.

Dog raised an eyebrow. "Indeed, sir. Shall we depart at once? The sooner we leave, the sooner we can save Lady Lysandra and Colin."

"We're rescuing the horses, not the people! Honestly, Dog. Sometimes I wonder about you. We'll reclaim my steeds and liberate Colin's, and then escape this insane mission. Cook the deer as quickly as possible, a man cannot be expected to be heroic on an empty stomach."

Whilst his manservant saw to the meal Sir Edric scoured the camp for weapons. Most of them had been with the horses, and he was disappointed to find only a pair of quarterstaffs. Still, he had his crossbow.

The venison was delicious, and after polishing it off Sir Edric and Dog started to track the horses. The trees were close to one another, and recently broken branches provided numerous signs of the brigands' route. The trail was longer than they might have expected, and Sir Edric began to worry about their provisions.

"We're down to the last two bottles of wine, Dog. We must make haste!"

They continued with renewed vigour and urgency, but unfortunately night soon fell, and Sir Edric refused to try and continue by torchlight.

"Hard to sneak up on someone if we're carrying a flaming torch in the dead of night, Dog. We'll sleep for a little while, and then resume our hunt before dawn. I'll take the first watch."

His manservant settled down for the night, and Sir Edric occupied himself dreaming up ways to torture the horse-thieves.

I could sell them to Orff. Or have them imprisoned in the Netherhole of Pung-Fek.

Come first light the pair continued tracking the broken branches through the dense forest, and soon came within earshot of a strange, jabbering conversation.

What a barbaric tongue. Sounds like a cat being put through a mangle.

Sir Edric crept along the ground, crossbow at the ready, and saw two peculiar creatures. They were scarcely three feet tall, rather chubby and covered in light grey fur. Their dinky snouts sprouted enormous white whiskers that wobbled as they sniffed the air. Neither carried a weapon, a foolish oversight that Sir Edric decided to take advantage of.

"Wait here, Dog," he ordered, before emerging from the undergrowth and accosting the furballs.

He levelled his crossbow at the nearest one. "Tell me where my horses are, you thieving swine."

"Uk duk, jiggly-noo," it replied.

The second raised its hands in surrender, or so Sir Edric thought. Moments later it flung a ball of fire at him and the knight was forced to leap out of the way.

The two strange little creatures chuckled and advanced upon him, hands raised to deal death. Eight feet of wood suddenly flew from the forest. Dog's quarterstaff sailed through the air and cracked the first creature on the temple. It crumpled to the ground, and whilst the second was distracted Sir Edric shot him in the groin.

"Splendid work, Dog," he congratulated his manservant.

After reloading, Sir Edric placed his boot on the agonised but still living creature's throat and aimed his crossbow at its head.

"Now, I do believe you were about to tell me where my horses are."

***

The strange furry sorcerer didn't seem to speak a word of any language Sir Edric knew, but had gestured frantically in a direction the knight assumed led to his horses. A quick blow to the head with a quarterstaff knocked the creature unconscious, enabling Sir Edric and Dog to pursue the stolen steeds without worrying about being pursued themselves.

The strange language soon reached their ears once again, and they crept through the undergrowth. Sir Edric crawled to the crest of a small hillock and saw beneath him a settlement. There were many untidy wooden huts and from the branches overhead skulls of humans, elves and Ursk dangled. At the opposite side of the settlement Sir Edric could just about make out stables housing the four horses. In the centre of the village there were two scorched wooden stakes, at the foot of which were two crispy carcasses, burnt beyond all recognition.

Such a pity she's dead. On the other hand, it'd be a greater pity if I were.

"It would appear Lady Lysandra and Colin the Adventurer are no more," Dog sadly observed.

She had such splendid legs. If only I had been able to get to know them better.

"Indeed, now we just need to retrieve the horses and we can escape. No more spectre of highly probable death, Dog."

"Unless we get killed trying to rescue the horses, sir."

"Fret not, I'm sure you'll be fine."

Sir Edric led Dog on a circuitous route to the other side of the village. Fortunately the stables were very near to the forest, raising Sir Edric's hopes of getting his horses back and escaping.

"Right, Dog. Go to the stables and bring the horses back. I'll stay here to keep watch and shoot anyone who looks like they've seen you."

Sir Edric crouched against a tree trunk, crossbow raised and ready to fire at once. He watched as Dog slithered forward, until someone smacked Sir Edric hard on the back of the head and everything became dark.

***

When he awoke it was night time, and he had a thumping headache. Making matters worse, a dozen furry mages were pounding drums and chanting noisily. His hands were tied behind his back, securing him to what he guessed was a stake. To his left Dog was similarly bound.

"Good evening, sir," the manservant said.

"No it bloody isn't!" Sir Edric snapped.

Several of the creatures approached the knight and his servant, and started piling logs and kindling at the base of their stakes.

Perhaps I should've brought Moloch. Anyone trying to steal him would've had their face bitten off.

A villager with a feathery face mask and walking with a staff carved into an eagle's head approached Sir Edric. Behind him was another villager, who was walking very gingerly indeed. He patted his crotch gently, and then pointed at the knight.

Dear gods, what are they planning to do to us?

"I suspect that's the fellow you shot, sir," Dog said, interrupting the lurid terrors that were coursing through Sir Edric's mind.

Ah. That's a relief.

"What an ungrateful sod. I could've killed him, but the knightly duty of mercy persuaded me to let him live."

Around the two men the mounds of wood and kindling had reached halfway up their thighs. The masked villager, whom Sir Edric assumed was the chief, clapped his hands and the workers who had been piling the wood scurried away. The drums and chanting fell silent.

"You, strangers," the chieftain spoke in a clumsy but recognisable accent. "Invade our forest. We burn you, we kill you."

"Now, now, I just want my horses back," Sir Edric said. "I am a man of peace."

The villager he had shot in the groin muttered something incomprehensible.

The chief thrust his staff menacingly at the knight. "You attack us. We kill you, when the fire-god comes to watch," he said, gesturing at the east.

"That's not true," Sir Edric protested. "I was simply searching for my horses, which I can't help but notice are in your village, when two of your kind attacked me. Filled with the spirit of charity, I let that ungrateful sod live," he added, nodding at the chap he had shot earlier.

The chief smacked him on the foot with his staff. "Lies! Noble Juklak never steal! We find poor horses all alone and bring them to be our friends. You come to steal and kill!"

The chief spat on the ground and strode away. All the villagers retired to their huts for the night, leaving Sir Edric and Dog alone in the darkness. A horse whinnied, and the sound brought a smile to the knight's face.

"I have a plan, Dog," Sir Edric whispered. "Our hands are bound, but we are not actually tied to the stakes. Therefore, we can rub the rope binding our wrists against the stake, and hope that the roughness of the wood chafes the rope and enables us to wear it down before the sun rises."

"Indeed, sir." Dog hesitated, and then said, "Or we could just use our dirks to cut the ropes."

It took a little straining for Sir Edric to bend his legs and twist his arms sufficiently to reach into his boot, a task made more difficult by the wood piled around his legs. His trusty dirk soon made short work of the ropes, and he saw that Dog had enjoyed similar success. He ran for the stables, but the chief had not left them unobserved after all. A sentry shrieked an alarm, and from every hut the savages poured, hands raised to hurl magical death. They surrounded him, and Dog. The chieftain emerged from the crowd and pointed his staff at them.

"Dishonour the fire-god, you have," he intoned. The other villagers were utterly silent as they listened to him. "Now you die."

A river of flame burnt across the village, setting half of the huts alight. Sir Edric, Dog and the strange folk turned to see an elven enchantress and an annoyingly alive Adventurer charging the villagers. The chief raised his staff in Lysandra's direction and Sir Edric kicked him in the nuts.

Caught between facing the blade of Colin, Lysandra's magic and the two former captives half a dozen of the villagers fell at once, and the rest fled into the forest.

"What are you doing here?" Sir Edric asked.

"What am I doing here? What are *you* doing here?" Lysandra demanded.

Rescuing my horses and fleeing to glorious freedom.

"I came to save *you*," Sir Edric responded.

For the first time the elf appeared lost for words and a strange expression appeared on her face.

That's an unfamiliar one... gratitude? No... something good though. Latent desire maybe.

"Hurrah for your knightly valour," Colin said. "We were captured by these magic-wielding scallywags but managed to escape. We went back to the camp and found yourselves and the horses missing, and surmised you had been captured. So, we came back to rescue you. Great minds think alike, eh?"

And fools are never far apart.

"Sir, might I suggest we depart before our antagonists return?" Dog said.

"Let us leave this place," Lysandra agreed.

"Wait a damned moment!" Sir Edric said, stopping the elf in her tracks. "We can't leave the horses in a burning village."

That strange expression appeared on her face a second time, but he had more important things to deal with. Sir Edric ran over to the stables, and checked that each horse appeared in good health. Thankfully the flames were on the far side of the village and the four horses were able to be led out quite calmly.

***

Lysandra's magic proved useful for a second time that night, to Sir Edric's amazement. It was perilous to wander through a forest in the darkness, but thanks to a ball of glowing light the elf summoned they were able to move safely. It was past dawn when they finally left the forest, and they decided simply to make a long day of it and continue riding.

When the time came to make camp they were all exhausted by the escapades of the previous night and the lengthy day. Nevertheless, Sir Edric was preparing to go hunting when Lysandra asked him to stay at camp.

"Dog, accompany Colin on his hunt," he ordered, adding more quietly, "And keep him away for as long as possible."

His manservant nodded knowingly, strolling off with Colin and leaving his master alone with Lysandra.

"I am quite amazed that you chose to enter the lion's den to try and save me," she said. "Had you simply left, you would have been free of your onerous burden."

I know. And now I feel like an utter fool.

Lysandra leaned towards him and kissed him on the cheek. "Thank you, Sir Edric."

Latent desire! I knew it!

"Why thank me? We didn't save you. You weren't even there."

She smiled at him. "Perhaps the deed was not accomplished, but your heart was in the right place."

Be subtle, Edric. She's very beautiful but as vicious as a stabbed rat.

He got up to put another log on the fire, and when he returned he sat rather nearer her. Yawning, he stretched his arms wide and put one of them around her shoulder. It took all his courage to stop himself tensing in preparation for the magical assault that might come his way, but instead Lysandra rested her head on his shoulder.

Sir Edric moved slightly, and she raised her head. He leaned in to kiss her-

"We're back! What an exciting hunt that was!" Colin shouted cheerily.

Lysandra got to her feet to help prepare the deer Dog was carrying over his shoulders, leaving Sir Edric alone by the fire.

Queen of Flames

It had taken some self-restraint on Sir Edric's part not to simply shoot Colin after the youth had managed to destroy his best chance of defrocking Lysandra. Happily, sparring provided a perfect excuse to give him a damned good thrashing. A swift quarterstaff to Colin's codpiece had made the knight feel better about his own being neglected.

The town beyond the Forest of Bones was named Revska, and was populated mostly by humans as well as the odd Ursk. Sir Edric, deprived of elven comfort and acutely aware of his impending doom, decided to generously support the town's economy by visiting the better of the two brothels. By the time he left the establishment he discovered that Dog had purchased some food and crossbow bolts, Colin had bought a map, and Lysandra had acquired a disapproving frown.

"Enjoy yourself?" she asked acidly after watching him leave the brothel.

"No."

The elf raised an eyebrow.

"If I wanted to enjoy myself I could do it for free. Enjoying other people is why I have to pay. And stop looking so bloody grumpy. I wouldn't have to divert my natural urges this way if you hadn't dragged me hundreds of miles away from my paramour."

Lysandra sighed. "Really? Dog and Colin aren't frequenting brothels."

He shrugged.

Of course they aren't. Dog doesn't have the money, and Colin wouldn't know one end of a woman from another. (And they really don't like that).

"Engaging in an adulterous relationship with the wife of the monarch is nothing to be proud of!"

He folded his arms. "You make it sound like a sordid affair. She was in an unhappy marriage, wed to a feeble, weak-kneed bedwetter, and I've never even consummated my marriage. We met one another, and a sympathetic fondness blossomed into true love. What we had was a deep, spiritual connection."

"What was her name?" Lysandra asked.

Shit.

"Her real name, not the regnal one she took when she got married."

A man can't be expected to remember every sodding detail...

Behind Lysandra, Dog mimed a capital A, and was halfway through a second pose when the elf turned around and he stopped abruptly.

"Amy," Sir Edric guessed confidently. A knight should always sound confident. It reassured uncertain followers and made enemies doubtful.

The surprised look on her face told him at once his answer was correct. She strode away, followed by a puppy-like Colin.

"Good show, Dog," Sir Edric thanked his manservant.

Dog bowed his head. "Indeed, sir."

***

The further north they rode the colder the climate grew. Grey clouds obscured the sun, and flakes of snow started to tumble. They saw no sign of civilisation, and the road dwindled rapidly until it disappeared altogether. Sir Edric was bemused when they passed several mounds of enormous bones, but glad that they appeared to be extremely old.

Whatever did this must be long gone. Hopefully.

"Are you sure we're going the right way?" Sir Edric asked. Except for some mountains in the far distance they were surrounded by nothing but a sea of grass.

Colin beamed a smile at him. "Oh, yes." The Adventurer unfurled his map and moved a little closer to the knight. "See? We're here," he said, pointing.

Sir Edric looked at the map, and then at Colin.

84

He's still smiling. Somewhere a village is missing its idiot.

"Here? Where it says 'Here there be dragons'?"

Colin nodded.

"No need to be scared, Edric," Lysandra interrupted. "That's just what cartographers write when they don't know what's there."

"Have you ever seen a dragon?" Colin asked, rolling his map back up and stowing it away.

"Yes, briefly. It was at the Battle of Lo-Kalzek. I was fighting under the banner of Duke Sigmund against the peasants, who were, as usual, revolting."

Colin seemed enthralled, despite Sir Edric's lack of enthusiasm for the subject. "Did the battle go well?"

It's not the greatest challenge to defeat some starved malcontents armed with pointy sticks when you're armoured from head to toe.

"The battle was hard fought, but thanks to our valour and fraternal loyalty we prevailed. It was a glorious victory, and the enemy were utterly vanquished. And then the dragon showed up and killed everyone."

Lysandra said, "Not everyone. You survived, after all."

I stole the Duke's horse and galloped away. The dragon was too busy eating nobility to notice.

"I am a man of uncommon courage and skill, but even so I recognise danger when I see it."

"I hope that one day I too have such tales to recite, when I reach my final years," Colin stated.

Keep talking like that and your final years might be closer than you think, you cheeky bastard.

Apart from the occasional bird flying high above and distant herds of mastodons they saw little alive in the grassland. The endless trek across the wilderness began to grate on Sir Edric's nerves. As he gradually plodded nearer the Unholy Temple time dragged painfully. It reminded him of sentry duty the night before battle. In many ways, it was worse than the fighting, for a man had nothing but his doubts and fears for company. Like reinserting a dislocated shoulder or ending a dalliance with a lady friend, it was better to just get it over with quickly.

The snow grew thicker, and as the sky darkened Lysandra suggested they camp for the night. Although hunting seemed a forlorn hope, Sir Edric and Dog decided to have a crack at it anyway. The knight was grateful of some time away from Colin's remorseless chirpiness, and it seemed that his prospects of bedding Lysandra had disappeared like a virgin in a brothel.

Unsurprisingly they saw nothing to hunt, but just as Sir Edric was turning back he heard an alarming noise. In the darkness, wings were beating. They sounded rather large.

"Does that sound like a dragon to you, Dog?"

His manservant pondered the question. "No, sir."

Thank the gods for that. The last thing I need is to be pursued by a fire-breathing winged reptile.

"Sounds more like a wyvern to me, sir," Dog said.

Suddenly Sir Edric felt a strong draught as the winged creature landed nearby. He shot at it, but his bolt veered into the darkness.

"Good evening," a deep voice said.

Sir Edric finished reloading his crossbow before replying. "Who are you?"

The creature took a few steps towards him, and even in the black of night its immense size and golden scales were apparent. Its head appeared to be larger than his entire body, and its reptilian eyes reflected brightly in the darkness.

A golden dragon. Splendid. My life expectancy has just become shorter than a gnome's todger.

"I am the Golden Dragon, the immortal Queen of Flames, the Ancient Terror. I was hatched before the world you know was born; I have flown in the skies for countless centuries. The walls of proud cities tumbled beneath my might and armies of your mortal kind bowed before me. My name has inspired fear and awe throughout the world. Gaze upon my glory and tremble, human, for I am Janet!"

I... Janet?

"Janet?" Sir Edric asked aloud, wondering if he had somehow misheard the thunderous words of the dragon.

The dragon sighed, producing a wave of air so strong it almost knocked him from his feet.

"You bloody humans. I'm an eternal wielder of primal magics, the mightiest dragon upon all the earth and all any of you ever bloody ask about is the name."

Deciding not to press the matter, he said, "Terribly sorry, I didn't mean to be rude. Er, can I help you?"

Janet gazed at him, and he found himself transfixed by her beautiful golden eyes. And then she burst out laughing, a tremendous sound that made him and Dog cover their ears.

"Help me? You? I think not. But *I* could help *you*. I can take you where you need to go."

Huzzah for the end of this tedious trek!

"And in return for this kind offer?" he asked cautiously. In Sir Edric's experience, even the most seemingly generous gift came with a cost.

"I ask only that you complete the task that has been given you. The Unholy Temple of Despair and Certain Doom lies within my territory, but has been infested with Ursk. I could destroy them, of course, but I do not wish to damage that ancient edifice," Janet explained. "And it would be nice to have some company. Very few people are brave or stupid enough to travel to a place marked 'Here there be dragons', you know."

Obviously. You'd have to be an utter cretin to do something like that.

Sir Edric had Dog run back to the campsite to fetch Lysandra and Colin, and stayed to chat with Janet. The dragon, apart from an almost elven level of self-regard, was rather likeable.

"Do you ever eat people?" Sir Edric asked.

"Oh, humans are easily my favourite to eat," Janet said. "Ursk are too tough and chewy, Fyntok fill my mouth with feathers and elves are nice but a bit on the skinny side. Give me a nice juicy human to eat any day. Well, several of them. A single one doesn't go very far. I am quite large, you know."

Dog returned, leading Lysandra and Colin. Upon seeing the dragon the Adventurer drew his sword, screamed a war cry and charged. Janet looked down, bemused, as Colin repeatedly slashed at her leg. His blade bounced off her golden scales and sparks flew.

Go on, stamp on the little bastard. You know you want to.

"I say, stop that," Janet said.

Colin refused. "Have at thee, foul beast! I shall slay you!"

"Colin!" Lysandra snapped. The Adventurer paused mid-swing and turned to look at the elf, who had her hands on her hips. "Knock it off."

Rather shame-faced, he sheathed his sword, mumbled an apology and joined the others.

"I don't suppose you know who's leading the Ursk?" Sir Edric asked.

"I believe a sorceress is their leader," Janet replied.

Oh goody. More magic... wait a minute! Magic doesn't work in the Unholy Temple! All I'll have to do is shoot her. Huzzah!

"Ha. I laugh in the face of sorceresses," Sir Edric said. He saw Lysandra scowling, and added, "Present company excepted, of course."

***

It turned out that flying was both deeply exhilarating and utterly terrifying. Dog and Colin had spent most of the early hours of the day with ropes, transforming their four tents into makeshift seats tied to the great horns that arose from Janet's back. Sir Edric and Lysandra had occupied themselves chatting with the dragon. The knight was very glad that he had thought to alleviate himself before the ride, otherwise he suspected he might have ruined his trousers.

"How are the horses, Dog?" Sir Edric asked, shouting to make himself heard over the noise of the air rushing past them.

Most of their goods could be secured within the tents or tied directly to Janet's many horns, but the horses had presented a slight problem. The dragon had offered to shrink the steeds until they were no larger than a squirrel, and then restore them once the Unholy Temple was reached. Sir Edric had volunteered Dog's tent as the best place to keep the miniature equines for the duration of the flight.

"I think their bladders are empty now, sir," Dog replied, the slightest hint of displeasure creeping into his otherwise neutral voice.

Sir Edric peered down at the distant land and almost yelped in fear. The grasslands were hurtling by at the gods alone knew what speed.

I wonder if I could persuade her to give me a lift back to Awyndel. A dragon landing on the castle is bound to impress the Queen, and petrify her husband.

At his behest his own tent and Lysandra's were next to one another, on the opposite side of Janet to Dog and Colin. The elf's golden hair was billowing freely in the wind, and in the bright sunshine she was heart-achingly beautiful.

"Look!" she shouted, pointing west.

Sir Edric turned his head and saw a V-formation of flying birds that drew closer, and as they did so he realised they were eagles. And not any ordinary eagles, but enormous, majestic birds, each one large enough to carry a man on its back.

Or in its talons.

He took a bolt and prepared to fire his crossbow, but Lysandra shook her head.

"The giant eagles are friends of all who are pure of heart," she said.

The eagles banked their wings and flew away from Janet, prompting a perfectly pretty sigh from Lysandra.

"I should've shot one of them," Sir Edric decided. "The head alone would be a trophy fit for a king. A proper king, I mean, not Lawrence."

"They're graceful and noble creatures, Edric. Many a time they have helped a poor man, or woman, in need."

Sir Edric laughed scornfully. "I'm in need, but they've never bloody helped me! Think how many unnecessary perils we've faced when we could've just flown all the way to the Temple."

During the journey the sky was far busier than he had expected. They passed a giant bat, a flock of harpies, and a flange of flying baboons.

"I wonder what evil they are doing," Lysandra commented as the red-bottomed winged primates flew past.

"Going back to Esmerelda, I imagine," Sir Edric replied.

A laggard baboon suddenly crashed into the side of Janet and snapped its jaws at Lysandra. Before she could do anything a crossbow bolt struck the beast in the shoulder and sent it hurtling to its doom.

Sir Edric began reloading his crossbow, but his attention was diverted by the beautiful elf reaching over and hugging him tightly. She kissed him on the cheek.

"Thank you, Sir Edric," Lysandra said. "You... you saved my life. I don't know how to thank you."

I have several ideas, actually.

***

Janet set them down a day's travel from the Unholy Temple, so that they could approach without being spotted. Her beating wings almost knocked Sir Edric off his feet, and then she serenely flew away. Thankfully the horses, having been restored to their usual size, appeared no worse for wear, and

90

before night fell they had covered half the distance towards the Temple.

"I shall pray for you," Lysandra told Sir Edric during supper. The pair were alone at the fire, for night had fallen and their companions had gone to sleep.

Well, it worked against Greymond.

"To be honest, I am keen to finish this quest," Sir Edric claimed. "The Temple's so close. I think it would be best if Dog and I scouted ahead to ensure the way is free of ambush."

And, if it is, we can gallop away to freedom.

"No, Edric. We've been through a lot together, and I shall see you safe to the Temple's gates."

Bugger.

His face fell, and he sighed.

Lysandra placed a hand on his and smiled at him. "If you are worried, then I think you underestimate yourself. Have you not faced and defeated numerous foes on our perilous journey here?"

She has a point. I am rather heroic. Who but me could have thwarted the necromancer Greymond, survived the deadly poison of an apothecary, freed Princess Manbeef from the Tower of Uz-Talrak or put up with Colin the Adventurer without throttling him to death?

"Maybe you're right."

That night dark and disturbing dreams troubled Sir Edric. After one particularly traumatic vision of Ganska Gro-Braful naked he decided it was wiser to simply stay awake. He checked and re-checked that his crossbow was in perfect working order, that his sword was sharper than lions' teeth and that all the wine was packed away, ready to be taken with them. As he had hours to wait until daylight, he decided to start work on one of the weaker bottles. He was rather enjoying it until Lysandra snatched the vessel from his lips.

"You can't fight if you're drunk," she nagged.

You've clearly never been on a battlefield. Or in a pub, for that matter.

"I am not drunk," he protested. "What a horrid slur. I'm merely sampling a little wine to stiffen the sinews and embolden the spirit."

The sun rose and bathed the depressingly near Unholy Temple of Despair and Certain Doom in golden light. It looked more like a citadel than a place of worship to Sir Edric's eyes, and was surrounded by a tall stone wall. The only way in was an open gateway beyond which was an overgrown garden. Lysandra travelled with them until that solitary entrance, and they dismounted.

"I can go no further," the sorceress said. "I shall look after your horses and wait here until either you emerge victorious or the wagons bearing the ransom arrive."

You might be waiting a while. I hope Grog got the lot.

"Lady Lysandra, thank you for your kindness and wisdom on our journey," Dog said.

She beamed with delight and gave the manservant a hug.

"Keep your master and yourself safe, Dog."

Colin the Adventurer next approached the elf. "Do not worry, dear Lys, for I am accompanied by the Hero of Hornska. If any man alive can return victorious from this place, it is he!"

Lysandra embraced the Adventurer and gave him a peck on the cheek. "Be cautious, Colin. Your boldness does you credit, but the Unholy Temple is a dangerous place."

The sorceress was kept waiting whilst Sir Edric finished off his bottle of wine and then discarded it. "Well, here we are. Highly probable death awaits me."

Lysandra smiled, though she looked rather forlorn. "Best of luck, Sir Edric," she said, holding her hand out.

He stared at it in disbelief.

A handshake? Even Dog got a bloody hug!

Well aware that there was a good chance he would be dead before sunset he took hold of the elf's hand, pulled her near and kissed her on the lips.

The Unholy Temple

It was slow going. The Unholy Temple was surrounded by what had once been a garden, but it had long since decayed into a tangled mess of overgrown weeds. Dog and Colin were forced to use their daggers to hack their way through the foliage, whilst Sir Edric staggered behind them. For a moment Lysandra had proved rather receptive to a game of tonsil tennis, up until the point at which she'd kneed him between the legs.

"Hold on a second," Sir Edric called.

Colin and Dog paused and looked back at the knight.

"Is it still painful, Sir Edric? Would you like me to rub some ointment into the bruise?" Colin asked.

"No, I bloody well would not!" he snapped. "I think I saw something moving. The Ursk might have posted scouts. Keep your eyes peeled."

Gradually the pain in his nethers began to recede, but as Dog and Colin were doing such a good job cutting through the undergrowth it seemed a shame to disturb them. Sir Edric instead busied himself watching carefully for any sign of violent red-skinned giants, but there were none to be seen. He rested for a moment, leaning against a tree trunk, when a flower near his hand swivelled around to face him.

What a charming little fellow.

"Good morning," Sir Edric greeted the flower.

Teeth protracted from the petals and the flower tried to bite him on the arm. Fortunately his sleeve took the brunt of the bite and he tore the pernicious plant in two and tossed it on the ground.

"Watch out, men. It seems that the garden is rather bloody-minded," he informed Dog and Colin.

"Indeed, sir," Dog called back.

Sir Edric turned to face them and saw that a pair of gigantic plants, each with a plethora of snapping flower-jaws, was advancing upon the two men. He scanned the dense garden quickly, and realised that more marauding monstrosities were drawing near.

We'll be surrounded! Unless…

"Follow me!" Sir Edric shouted.

He clambered up the tree trunk until he reached the thickest limb that could support his weight. Sir Edric carefully walked along it, using his hands to grip the limb, and then leapt with all the grace of a drunken octopus towards the next nearest tree. His face crashed into it, but he managed to hold onto the trunk. Several more ungainly jumps enabled him to not only escape the murderous Magnolia but clear the garden altogether.

Dog soon followed him, and Colin likewise.

"Huzzah!" Sir Edric cheered.

Dog coughed politely. "I am afraid that whilst we are out of the garden, sir, we are not yet out of the woods."

Behind the three men, and between them and the Unholy Temple, a horde of slow but relentless plants had assembled. He fired his crossbow at the nearest, but the bolt merely ruffled a few petals and made the flower a little less pretty.

What a way for a hero to die. Mauled to death by vengeful vegetables.

"Sir, the wine!" Dog exclaimed.

"Good thinking, Dog," Sir Edric replied, lifting a bottle to his lips. The deep red beverage definitely made him feel better.

His manservant said, "Actually, sir, I meant that if we could stuff a rag into the neck then set it alight we could use the bottles as makeshift incendiaries."

Bloody hell. I didn't expect sobriety to be one of the ordeals I faced.

Working frantically, the men tore the pack that had held the wine bottles into rags, and followed Dog's plan.

"But how are we to light it?" Colin asked as the bloodthirsty botany shuffled closer.

Sir Edric undid the straps on his own pack and plunged a hand inside. Moments later it emerged clutching a tinderbox and pipe. He took the time to light the pipe, and tossed the tinderbox to Dog.

And to think Lysandra said smoking was bad for me.

Dog lit the first rag and used that to set the others ablaze. He handed the first bottle to Sir Edric.

"Time for some roast vegetables," he said before hurling the bottle hard at the nearest plant. The glass shattered and the wine exploded into a fireball.

Dog and Colin threw the other bottles, and soon the grisly garden was engulfed in a roaring conflagration that reduced it to ash.

"Well, that's the wine gone," Sir Edric said with a sigh. "We had better make haste. I shall not suffer sobriety longer than I must."

The Unholy Temple was a massive, imposing building more akin to a fortress than a place of worship. Towering walls rose as forbiddingly as any castle, and no stained glass provided a colourful relief from the bleak grey stone. Gruesome gargoyles weathered by the elements and time prowled along the walls. Windows, empty of glass or shutters, were small and defensible, and there appeared to be only a single entrance.

Between Sir Edric and the front doors of the massive structure a tall warrior stood. A bright golden mask with holes for eyes and mouth covered his face, and he was clad in black steel armour. Four arms sprouted from his body, and each one held a sword that glinted in the morning sun.

"Strangers, you are not welcome in this place," the warrior proclaimed.

"Yes, I gathered that when the garden tried to eat me," Sir Edric replied.

The warrior peeled back its lips in a ghoulish smile. "I am versed in the Nine Arts of Elven Swordcraft, the Unspoken Whisper of Lo-Kalzek, the Mystic Blade of the Arcane and the Paladin's Red Hand Style. You cannot hope to stand before my swordsmanship. Prepare to die!"

Sir Edric raised his crossbow and shot him in the head.

"I'm not sure that's strictly in accordance with the rules governing duels," Colin the Adventurer observed.

Sir Edric wandered a little closer towards the Temple's doors, and stopped. Countless bones were strewn upon the ground, some of them whole and many of them snapped in two or shattered into fragments.

He held a hand up to halt his companions. "Something's not right here."

Sir Edric picked up a nearby skull and tossed it at the door. A bolt of lightning erupted from a dragon carved into the wall and the bone shattered into tiny fragments.

"Dear gods!" Colin said. "We would surely have been killed if we had taken a few more steps."

I should see about getting one of those to deter travelling salesmen. And heralds.

Sir Edric puffed on his pipe. "We haven't even gone inside yet and we've already come across three lethal obstacles." He peered at the walls of the Unholy Temple. "We could always try climbing up and going in through a window."

Dog said, "Perhaps, sir. There are numerous gargoyles to use as purchase, but there's every chance the wall is protected by violent magical traps."

That's a good point.

"Colin, your bravery and skill has impressed me. I grant you the honour of going first. Take a rope, ascend to the nearest window and then drop it down so myself and Dog can climb up."

The Adventurer seemed delighted at being selected as the most expendable man present, and saluted smartly. "Thank you, Sir Edric. I shall endeavour to prove worthy of being the vanguard."

Ah, the vanguard. Such a fancy word for describing the people most likely to end up dead.

Colin successfully reached the window, and soon tossed down a rope. Sir Edric handed his own pack to Dog, and waited as his servant climbed up. Despite his encumbrance Dog made swift work of it, and his master followed quickly.

They were in a cramped corridor, barely large enough for two men to walk abreast. Not a single inch of stonework was bare; every part of the walls, floor and ceiling had been engraved with straight-edged runes. Dog was examining some of the ancient text with great interest.

Sir Edric relit his pipe, put it in his mouth and sputtered with shock as a shower of water gushed down onto his head. It matted his hair and soaked his clothes as well as extinguishing his pipe.

"What the hell's going on?" the soggy knight demanded.

"Well, sir," Dog replied, not taking his eyes away from the wall. "I believe it's a particularly archaic form of High Seleucian. This section describes prohibited acts within the Temple. Magic is forbidden, as is nudity, drunkenness and smoking."

Sir Edric scowled. "The architect sounds like a miserable bugger."

Probably an elf.

"It says here," Dog continued, studiously ignoring the saturated state of his master, "that the Keeper of the Temple, the steward of its great power, holds the sacred seals and sceptre. Surely that cannot refer to the royal treasures we seek?"

Sir Edric, despairing of relighting his pipe, flung it out of the window. "If that's a coincidence then I'm a monkey's uncle. What are these great and terrible powers, beyond half-drowning a man for having the temerity to enjoy a smoke?"

Dog cleared his throat and gestured at the runes covering every inch of the walls in the corridor, which stretched for some distance in either direction. "I might be able to find it, sir, but it would take me quite some time."

Sir Edric decided it was wiser to find and retrieve the royal treasures as rapidly as possible, and so the three men made their way along the corridor. There was neither sight nor sound of the Ursk, which was a pleasant surprise. Eventually they came to an empty doorway, beyond which was an enormous chamber. Four giant bronze statues, each one a hundred feet high, resided in the corners of the grand hall. They were all down on one knee, and braced the weight of the lofty ceiling upon their broad metal shoulders. Each held their arms straight out along the junction of the wall and ceiling, and grasped the hands of their neighbouring statues. Flaming braziers illuminated the hall and the quartet of metal giants who dwelt within it.

"These are magnificent!" Colin exclaimed, his voice echoing in the cavernous chamber. "Why, if they stood up they'd cause the roof to cave in."

Sir Edric, recalling the golem in the Forest of Bones, decided it would be best to hurry on. A large doorway led away from the grand hall, but if anything it made him feel even more uncomfortable. Lining the long, straight corridor were countless stone statues, each one exquisitely carved and eight feet tall. They appeared to be warriors, clutching morning stars and falchions, shields and axes. Blazing torches were ensconced between the statues, their flames casting dancing shadows upon the stone sentinels. There was no sign of movement, but Sir Edric felt as if scores of beady eyes were staring at him. At the end of the corridor was a slab of stone covered with runes.

"Have a quick read, Dog," Sir Edric commanded.

I wish I had some wine to pass the time. Or my pipe. Curse this monument to asceticism.

Colin attempted to strike up a conversation, but the knight ordered him to be silent in case the Ursk heard him.

Not that I want to hear him either.

After much reading Dog finally reported that the stone slab was a door, but a strange one. "It appears to have some sort of magical property, sir. It's not a trap," he added, "but it will only open for a man of true blood."

Sir Edric asked, "Meaning?"

Dog frowned. "I'm not entirely sure, sir. It could be a reference to virtue, or being born to married parents."

"This place was designed by a puritanical buffoon. What sort of imbecile would make doors work based on someone's supposed virtue? Anyway, I grow tired of being surrounded by statues. Open it, Dog."

The manservant nodded, and placed both hands upon the door. He pushed gently, and then hard, and grunted with the effort, but the door was very unco-operative. Sir Edric gestured at Colin, who eagerly moved to assist Dog, but even with both men straining every sinew they could not move the hefty stone an inch. After some time the two men, both breathing hard with their exertion, relented.

"Bugger," Sir Edric said. "We'd better go back and try and find some other way to reach the seals."

"Could we possibly have a rest?" Colin asked.

So much for the vigour of youth.

"Fine."

Dog and Colin sat on the ground, and Sir Edric cast his eye over the runes covering the door. The straight-edged letters were utterly indecipherable and he soon despaired of finding anything of use. He leant against the door, and fell backwards when his weight forced it open.

"Of course, true blood must refer to Sir Edric's knightly status," Colin said.

Of course. I wish he'd thought of that before I bruised my backside.

Sir Edric got to his feet, dusted himself down and led them deeper into the Temple. Eventually they came to a spiral staircase.

He listened intently but could hear nothing coming from above or below. The knight tapped the runes by the stairs and had Dog translate them.

"It says that the dungeon is below, and the House of Treasures is above. On the roof," Dog reported.

Sir Edric ordered Colin to go first and followed, crossbow at the ready, right behind him. The three men emerged onto the large roof, in the middle of which a circle of stone pillars surrounded a small altar. Sir Edric, sensing no Ursk nearby, peered around a column at the altar and spotted what looked like several round seals and a long sceptre resting upon it. He strolled towards the royal treasures.

"I'm delighted you've made it this far," a woman crooned at him.

The knight raised his crossbow and scanned the roof. From behind a pillar a woman with a long, pointy nose and more warts than a toad's backside walked.

And to think she's the prettiest of her sisters.

"Neptunia?" Sir Edric asked, wondering if he'd remembered her name correctly and not bothering to lower his crossbow. "We all know magic doesn't work in here. You can surrender if you like, or shall I simply shoot you in the head?"

Neptunia cackled. "There aren't any runes on the roof, Edric."

A shockwave erupted from her fingertips and hurled Sir Edric hard against one of the pillars. He landed roughly on his crossbow, which fired a bolt straight into his thigh. The knight screamed in agony. He looked up from the ground and saw that Colin had fallen and appeared to be unconscious. Of Dog there was no sign.

"Dog?" Sir Edric called.

Nobody answered.

Sir Edric forced himself into a sitting position and began reloading his crossbow. "You fiend! Do you have any idea how hard it is to find a good manservant?"

"Aww, poor Edric. Never you-" Neptunia paused mid-sentence when he shot his crossbow. The witch plucked the bolt from the air and laughed. "Such a feisty boy. Sleep now. You must be well rested, for the next morning shall be your last!"

Try as he might to resist, his eyes became heavy and he slumbered.

***

Sir Edric opened his eyes, and soon came to the conclusion that doing so was a mistake. He was locked in a large cell with Colin the Adventurer, and his leg hurt so much it reminded him of the time a copper bee had stung him in the crotch. Hopefully this time the wound would not take a surgeon, tweezers and two hours of painful probing to rectify. One wall of the cell consisted of thick iron bars, beyond which two Ursk were playing cards at a table.

"Sir Edric, we've been captured!" Colin remarked.

Thank you, Colin. I had noticed that.

The knight tentatively patted his thigh, and instantly regretted it. Burning, fiery pain met his gentle touch and he had to grit his teeth to stop himself crying out.

"Does it hurt?" Colin asked.

"I was shot in the leg with a crossbow, you berk, of course it bloody hurts!"

"Is there anything I can do to help?" Colin asked.

"You could shut up."

The Adventurer nodded, but denied Sir Edric blissful silence anyway. "Who was that woman?"

"Neptunia, a foul witch, an appallingly ugly creature and a worker of the darkest magics. She's also my sister-in-law. Still, she's better than that rotten hag Esmerelda."

"But she's your wife!" Colin protested. "Surely Esmerelda must have some virtues?"

Sir Edric considered the matter for a moment. "Mortality."

He reached down and checked the inside of his boot. To his dismay his trusty dirk had been taken.

"We need a plan. You lay down and pretend to be dead. When they open the cell, knock them out and we shall make our heroic escape," Sir Edric explained in a murmur.

Colin nodded enthusiastically and then closed his eyes and lay perfectly still.

"Oh no!" Sir Edric shouted. "My dear friend Colin is surely dead!"

He looked across at the Ursk, neither of whom had got up from the table.

"Dead! Surely you must find out if he is or not, and then tell that wretched crone who paid you to guard him?" Sir Edric said.

One of the Ursk tossed a coin into the middle of the table and took another card from the deck. "Nah, she's only bothered about you. So long as you're alive to torture later she's happy."

That's a comforting thought.

"So... if she's not bothered about Colin why don't you eat him?" Sir Edric suggested. "Be a shame to waste a good fresh corpse, wouldn't it?"

The hulking carnivores evidently agreed, for they rose from the table and unlocked the iron door. The pair approached Colin, who kicked one of them in the knee. The second Ursk caught the Adventurer in a tight grip, his bulging arm muscles locked around Colin's neck.

Sir Edric tried to run for the open door, but his wounded leg reduced him to hobbling. The Ursk Colin had kicked recovered in plenty of time to block his way.

"Neptunia needs you alive, but she won't care if you have a broken bone or two," the carnivore snarled. It unsheathed its wickedly curved sword and bared its fangs.

The plan has developed in a way which is not necessarily to my advantage.

Realising his chances of beating the warrior in a fight were smaller than a banker's heart, Sir Edric drew himself up to his full height and said, "Oh, you ignorant and feeble creature! Perhaps an ordinary man might be afraid of a dim-witted, knuckle-dragging brute, but I am Sir Edric Greenlock, the Hero of Hornska! If you relinquish your blade and stand aside I may be willing to let you live, but if not then I shall strangle you with your own entrails. Surrender or die!"

There is absolutely no chance of this working. I should've tried kicking him in the nuts. That always works. Nobody can withstand their goolies being pulverised.

The Ursk yelped in terror and fell to its knees.

Yes! Kneel before the ferocious Hero of Hornska, puny Ursk!

It was then that Sir Edric noticed a small metal point protruding from the middle of the brute's chest. The blade was withdrawn and Dog decapitated the Ursk with a single perfect stroke of his sword.

"Dog... you're alive!" Sir Edric exclaimed.

"Indeed, sir," his manservant replied. "And so are you. Ought I intervene on Colin's behalf?" he asked.

The Adventurer was trying to grapple with the monstrous strength of the warrior holding him, without much success. His face had turned a deep purple.

Sir Edric sighed. "I suppose so."

One elegant thrust of Dog's sword later the Ursk lay dead and Colin was gasping for breath and attempting to offer his thanks.

"How did you survive?" Sir Edric demanded.

Dog had indeed been blown from the roof by the force of Neptunia's magic. He had landed upon the hard ground, he explained, broken both legs and one arm, and used his sole functioning limb to drag himself outside. There Lysandra had healed him, and he had returned to either save or revenge his master.

"Bravo!" Colin cheered the manservant's pathological loyalty.

Dog led them from the prison and up some stairs, where a guard he had killed earlier was marinated in his own blood. In a little room beyond were their packs and weaponry. Sir Edric opted only for his dirk and crossbow, as his wound would make it difficult to bear a heavier burden.

"To the roof!" the knight declared. His leg still hurt, but the prospect of reclaiming the treasures and escaping alive spurred him on.

Dog led the way as quickly as his master's hobbling gait could bear. Numerous Ursk were slain as they went until they came to the staircase that led to the rooftop. A veritable horde of the bloodthirsty red-skinned warriors charged down the narrow corridor at the three men.

"Never fear, sir," Dog said. "I shall see them off and protect your rear. Pray, go to the roof, and I shall hold them off until you can return."

Huzzah for you, Dog. My rear has never been in better hands.

At Sir Edric's order Colin led the way to the roof, whilst behind him he heard the clash of steel on steel.

Night had fallen, and it was rather chilly. Sir Edric spoke quietly to Colin, suggesting that the Adventurer sneak around one way whilst he went the other. Neptunia was in the middle of the circle of pillars, sat cross-legged and muttering some sort of chant.

"I see you," she crooned.

Sir Edric hid behind a column, crossbow poised.

"And I see you, vile witch," Colin proclaimed in his worst holier-than-thou voice. "Prepare to meet thy end!"

Sir Edric chanced to peer around the corner of the pillar just in time to see the Adventurer charging towards Neptunia. She hurled a purple bolt of lightning at him, but before it hit he threw his sword at her. The lightning struck him in the chest and sent him tumbling backwards, and his blade pierced

Neptunia's torso. She slumped to the ground, and smoke rose from Colin's body.

Sir Edric approached the witch very carefully, crossbow pointing at her head the whole time. She appeared dead, and he shot her in the forehead for good measure. A sudden thought came to him, and he pulled free Colin's blade and wiped it clean of blood before tossing it aside.

"Uh...." Colin groaned.

I wish he was always this quiet. He should get electrocuted more often.

"Quiet, Colin. Speaking now could risk straining yourself. Your recovery depends upon being absolutely silent."

The Adventurer struggled to sit up and nodded his understanding. He pointed at the corpse of Neptunia.

"Neptunia, the foul crone, is dead. Unfortunately your sword was wide of the mark, but thankfully your incompetence distracted her long enough for me to shoot her in the head," he explained.

Little Sacrifices

Sir Edric looked around for the royal treasures, and was delighted to see that the seals and sceptre remained on the altar. He strolled over and sighed with relief to finally collect them. The seals were carved circles of wood about the size of his palm. Each was engraved with intricate leaves, trees and forest animals. The serpent sceptre was rather more impressive. It was a shaft of ebony about five feet long around which a serpent of solid gold coiled. At the top of the staff the snake bared its fangs, and exquisite ruby eyes shone. A brief attempt to prise loose the rubies proved vain, and he reluctantly desisted.

All this for a few wooden discs and a snakey-stick.

He had just about finished stuffing the seals into his pack when Dog, soaked in blood from head to toe, arrived on the roof.

"Dog, you're filthy. The moment we reach a stream you're having a wash."

"Yes, sir. Is Colin alive?" he asked, looking at the prone and slightly smoking body of the Adventurer.

"Yes. Well, I imagine so. Unfortunately his terrible wound means he has to be absolutely still and silent. Any more Ursk?"

Dog shook his head, spraying droplets of blood from his hair. "No, I believe I slew them all."

Splendid. Back home for glory and adultery.

Sir Edric ordered Dog to tie a rope around the pillar nearest the edge of the roof so that they could climb down. Thankfully it just about reached the ground. Colin, grimacing with pain, wrapped his arms around Dog and the manservant climbed down as gently as he could. The effort and pain reduced the Adventurer almost to tears. Sir Edric's descent was not without difficulty, for his thigh still hurt terribly. When he reached the ground he was astounded to see a Royal Guardsman giving Colin some medical attention.

"What are you doing here?" the knight asked.

"The Ursk have us surrounded," the medic answered, rubbing some sort of cream on Colin's crispy chest. "We've had to use the wagons to barricade the gateway, but there must be a hundred of them."

What an ironic way to die. If I'd never told Grog about the wagons... wait a minute...

"I believe I have a plan to defeat our savage and terrible foe," Sir Edric stated. "Who is in command?"

I bet it's Drayton. Drayton or Malthus. Those preening, insufferable wretches will be gutted to see I'm still alive.

"Lieutenant Corkwell, sir," the medic answered. "She's over by the gate, organising the defence."

"What happened to your captain?"

The medic sighed. "The captain was blown to smithereens when he tried walking into the temple and was struck by a bolt of lightning. Lord Drayton was originally in command, but he was captured by the Ursk."

Sir Edric clenched his jaw to prevent himself from grinning.

I wonder if they've eaten him yet?

"Colin, let the medic look after you. Dog, with me."

Sir Edric strolled around the Temple towards the gateway, and was delighted to be met by two old friends when Temper and Twenty-Six trotted over. He patted Temper's snout and then let his trusty steed take the weight of his pack.

The camp was still in the process of being established. Only a handful of fires had been lit, around which several Guardsmen, old and young, had congregated. The youngsters were boasting bravely about all the grand deeds they would accomplish in the coming battle. The old hands were doing the old rituals, running whetstones over steel and murmuring prayers to the gods.

Before approaching the command tent, notable for its ludicrously over-sized flag, Sir Edric hunted down the quartermaster and requisitioned some wine. After finishing the second bottle he felt suitably revitalised and meandered towards the command tent.

Inside, a short, blonde woman was snapping orders at several sergeants, who ran off to do her bidding.

She looks familiar...

"Hello, stranger," Lieutenant Corkwell greeted him. She smiled and gave him a peck on the cheek. "I thought we might find you here."

"I must admit to being surprised to see you," he confessed, racking his brains to try and remember when they had last met. "I thought the wagons weren't due for weeks?"

Corkwell raised an eyebrow. "Drayton set the convoy moving the same day as you left, and moved so fast he half-killed the horses. He wanted to reach here before you did. Daft sod. He got his comeuppance, though. When the Ursk attacked near Northtown his horse was so exhausted it couldn't get away, and they captured him." She took a pair of bottles from underneath the table and tossed one to him. "Going to help in the defence, I take it?"

I like her.

Sir Edric had a little drink, and replied, "Better than that. I hope to negotiate for the Ursk to leave."

Corkwell laughed. "You must be drunk. The Ursk know we still have a king's ransom in gold. They'll never leave us." She sighed. "That pretty little elf you've been travelling with said she'd go and find some reinforcements for us. Wittered on about the eagles helping her, or somesuch nonsense. How'd you put up with her?"

She does have splendid thighs.

"Colin's worse," Sir Edric said. "Look, let me and Dog go and speak with the leader of the Ursk. It won't cost you anything, and you know they respect me because of the Battle of-"

"Hornska, yeah, we all bloody know what happened twenty years ago," Corkwell interrupted. "Fine. Just make sure you sort out a password and countersign with the men guarding the gate, or they might shoot you if you come back when it's dark."

I don't think coming back will prove a problem.

***

It was twilight when Sir Edric and Dog squeezed their horses through the gap between the two wagons blocking the gateway. Once they were through the wagons were rolled back to form an unbroken barricade.

"It's a shame I didn't get to spend some more time with Lieutenant Corkwell," Sir Edric said. "But we have a royal mission to accomplish."

"Indeed, sir."

The Ursk were encamped half a mile from the gate. A ring of captured wagons spoke of their initial success in ambushing the convoy, and a crude but sturdy pen had been built to keep their slaves from escaping. A score of fires were dotted around the camp and, as was normal for the Ursk, there were no sentries.

"Good evening," Sir Edric shouted. Wandering into an Ursk camp uninvited and unannounced was as dangerous as forgetting the King's birthday present, and he had no intention of being brutally murdered for violating etiquette.

Several of the nearest Ursk looked at him askance, until they noticed Dog's presence, lowered their eyes and shuffled away. A few moments later Grog Bel-Rot strode forward to greet the knight.

"Edric! Imagine my surprise to discover you were telling the truth," Grog said.

"Quite. Imagine my surprise when you didn't throw me out of the window."

Grog laughed, and Temper shied away from the carnivore's gruesome grin. "So, what're you doing here?"

"Shopping, actually. You don't happen to have a slave called Drayton, do you?"

110

Grog had a little think. "Fat bugger? Smells of cheese?"

Sir Edric nodded.

The Ursk fetched Drayton, who was bound hand and foot. He had lost rather a lot of weight, although his cheesy odour was sadly undiminished by captivity.

"Edric! I was rather hoping you'd be dead by now," the Lord Chamberlain said. He spat at the knight, who dodged the flying phlegm.

Ah, Drayton. Charming as a fungal infection.

"Dead? Me? If the ten thousand Ursk at Hornska couldn't manage it then the ragtag band of ragamuffins and scallywags in the Temple stood little hope." Sir Edric crouched beside the bound captive. "Speaking of which, it really was quite a coincidence that my sister-in-law was the one behind the theft. What's really going on here, Drayton? The Keeper and the seals are connected somehow, aren't they?"

Lord Chamberlain Drayton laughed. "And why should I tell you anything, weasel-knight?"

"Well, I was planning on buying your freedom from Grog. Still, if you insist on being obnoxious I could always have Dog bring the plum-crushers. I'm sure they'll help to squeeze the information out of you."

Drayton's beady eyes narrowed even more as he considered the offer. "You give me your word?"

"Cross my heart."

The royal seals of Awyndel were originally artefacts from the ancient world, Drayton explained. Legend said that the Keepers of the Holy Temple, as it was then known, were the guardians of its immense power. Should a Keeper be slain and his life blood bathe the seals then the Temple's gargoyles and statues would become golems, immune to magic and answerable only to the holder of the seals.

"Neptunia discovered that *you* were the heir to the Keepers," Drayton claimed. "We planned to marry, after using the army of invincible golems to conquer Awyndel."

111

Marry Neptunia? I'd sooner marry Dog.

"So, the King didn't send me here because I'm sleeping with his wife?" Sir Edric asked.

Drayton's jaw dropped.

Huzzah! I'll be able to carry on where I left off. On the other hand, if the King doesn't know, I can't very well take Drayton back with me now. He's bound to spill the beans to Lawrence...

"By the gods... the Queen's young, charming and beautiful. Why on earth is she sleeping with you?"

"Why shouldn't she? I'm young, charming and handsome. We're a perfect match."

"You're an arrogant forty-something still living off the memories of a battle from decades ago."

"Fine words, coming as they do from a slimy, conniving traitor. Now, are you going to tell me why Lawrence sent me on this mad mission, or shall I leave you in the tender clutches of Grog Bel-Rot?"

Disgust twisted Drayton's flabby face, but necessity obliged him to answer. He sighed in resignation, and Sir Edric wrinkled his nose in disgust as the cheesy odour of Drayton's breath polluted the air. "We told the King that Neptunia hated you, which happens to be true, and would return the seals in return for sending you to be horrifically tortured. The ransom was a means for us to get rich quick, sent by Lawrence in case you managed to abscond. That's why he sent the elf to escort you. But we never expected the Ursk to ambush us. The gods alone know how they found out about the wagons."

"Well, that all makes sense. Very well, I shall buy your freedom," Sir Edric promised.

He wandered over to Temper and rummaged through the panniers to find the gold Boris had given him. Sir Edric beckoned Grog over and dropped a ruby-encrusted golden ring into the Ursk's enormous clawed hand.

"Could you deliver him to a friend of mine?" Sir Edric asked.

"For a price."

The knight sighed and handed over another exquisite trinket. "Matriarch Vellia, in the Queendom of the Blue Forest."

Grog laughed. "Isn't that the place where they geld slaves?"

"Is it?" Sir Edric asked. "Given Drayton tried to have me tortured and killed he should be damned grateful he's only losing his plums. He'll be well looked after and perfectly safe."

"And a eunuch."

"We all have to make little sacrifices."

***

Sir Edric and Dog rode south, leaving behind the Unholy Temple, Colin the Adventurer and the Royal Guards.

I wonder when I'll get Hamilton's Trousers back.

"You seem deep in thought, sir. Worried about Lieutenant Corkwell?"

"Very concerned, Dog. By the way, she seemed to remember me, but she didn't ring a bell."

"You were intimately acquainted several years ago, sir, until you caught the Elven Flu. Whilst you were sick she was reassigned and had to leave without saying goodbye."

Damn. I should've tried my luck before leaving her.

"Do you think the Royal Guards will survive, sir?"

Sir Edric pondered the question a moment. "I'm sure they will, Dog. The Ursk are always after more slaves."

The two men rode along in silence, and it was almost entirely dark when they unexpectedly came across lots of soldiers, led by an elf.

"Sir Edric?" Lysandra asked, incredulous.

Oh, shit.

"Hello," he replied cautiously.

"Thank the gods you managed to escape from the Ursk," the elf said.

"Yes, huzzah for the gods!" he enthusiastically agreed. "Colin is seriously wounded, and I was overwhelmed with concern for him. Therefore, I sought to find you, or any other reinforcements, and urge you to make all haste!"

"Will you fight with us, Sir Edric?" one of the soldiers, whom he noted were wearing the uniform of Nurkabr, asked.

No. I've already saved your entire bloody kingdom and I am not going back to that infernal deathtrap.

"Alas, I have already been grievously wounded. Whilst battling a witch I was shot in the thigh with a crossbow bolt."

Lysandra edged towards him, and started to stroke her hands along his leg. Just as he was enjoying it a golden glow emanated from her hands and the pain in his leg vanished. She looked up at him and smiled.

You utter tease.

"It would mean a lot to me, Sir Edric, if you would fight with us," Lysandra said, pleading in that annoyingly irresistible voice women deploy on special occasions.

Damn it. I hope your definition of 'a lot' is the same as mine.

"Very well then. Come, men, we shall crush the puny Ursk once again!"

The eagles, Lysandra told Sir Edric, had helped carry the men of Nurkabr north, which was how they had managed to cover so much ground so swiftly. Sir Edric cursed the feathery bastards under his breath, and used the short journey back north to concoct a cunning scheme that would ensure total victory.

"The plan is simple. I shall lead the attack. The men of Nurkabr will follow as I charge. I want you," he said to Lysandra, "to sneak up to the Royal Guards and tell Lieutenant Corkwell to attack when she hears a battle break out."

Elves were stealthy by nature, and whether by art or magic Lysandra safely made it into the grounds of the Unholy Temple. As agreed with Lysandra beforehand, the Royal Guard placed several blazing torches atop the wall so that Sir Edric knew they would support his attack.

"Over two decades ago the Ursk were poised on the edge of victory over your kingdom," Sir Edric told the assembled ranks of the soldiers. It was important to give a pre-battle speech. It made the commander look like he knew what he was doing and made the chaps about to die feel like it might be worth it.

"Due to unstinting courage and the favour of the gods that foul red tide was turned back. Most of you were too young to take part, but luckily you'll get to wet your blades today. The Ursk aren't expecting an attack, and between us and the Royal Guard they'll be crushed in a vice of steel. Follow the flaming torch I carry," he said, raising it high, "and you shall know victory. Huzzah!"

"Huzzah!" the soldiers chanted back.

In the black of night the torch was the only thing visible, save for the camp's fires. Sir Edric and Dog trotted forward, leading the foot soldiers until they were within charging distance of the camp. The two horsemen were some way ahead of the soldiers.

Now for the most important part of the plan.

"Hold this, Dog," Sir Edric said, handing the torch to his manservant.

Dog sighed. "Indeed, sir. It's just like old times."

Twenty-Six surged into a gallop, and Sir Edric took Temper off to the side. The flaming torch was carried into the heart of the Ursk camp and then Dog threw it aside. War cries echoed as the soldiers followed the manservant, and then the clash of steel and screams of death filled the air. From the Unholy Temple the Royal Guardsmen charged, and the Ursk were massacred.

Sir Edric waited patiently, crossbow ready and eyes sharp. Once or twice an Ursk attempted to flee and he rode after the lumbering giant before burying a bolt between their shoulder blades. Otherwise, he spent the battle in perfect safety.

After the bloodletting had ended he searched for both Grog and Drayton. Happily, the Lord Chamberlain appeared to be missing, which suggested he was well on the way to having his goolies lopped off in a distant land. The absence of Grog was more worrying. He doubted the Ursk would have escorted

Drayton himself, and the fact his corpse wasn't to be found suggested he might yet live to exact revenge.

Colin the Adventurer had been more or less healed by Lysandra. When this had restored him to his usual state of verbal diarrhoea he had told the elf of Sir Edric's heroics defeating the witch Neptunia. The four travellers and Lieutenant Corkwell celebrated the victory in the command tent and toasted the knight.

"I've got to admit, I thought you'd just legged it," Corkwell told Sir Edric.

"I forgive you."

After all, I thought much the same.

"I shall travel with you as far as Nurkabr," Colin said. "I'm sure more adventures await me there, and King Boris will be eager to hear all about the terrible dangers and deadly foes we have faced."

Sir Edric finished off one goblet of wine and had Dog pour him another. "Oh, yes, I'm sure he will. Better not miss anything out, Colin. Perhaps you should compose a song you could sing him about it?"

"That's a brilliant idea, Sir Edric!" Colin agreed.

Pleading tiredness, he thanked Corkwell for the wine and turned in for the night. Along the way he checked to see how well-guarded the gold wagons were. Understandably, the Guardsmen were celebrating their survival and victory, affording him the opportunity to shovel several pounds of gold into his pack.

Tomorrow, the long ride home begins.

Manacled and Flogged

"It strikes me as rather strange, Dog," Sir Edric remarked.

It was nearing dusk, and the sun was setting prettily over Northtown. The knight had acquired the most expensive room in what passed for the town's best tavern and was enjoying a drink before bed.

"What does, sir?"

Sir Edric put his pipe in his mouth and lit up. Lysandra, of course, was sleeping in another room and Colin had left them in Nurkabr. Without her hectoring or Colin's endless wittering he was enjoying the rare opportunity to smoke in peace.

"On the way to the Unholy Temple we encountered all manner of terrible foes and unexpected peril. A necromancer, a murderous apothecary, a princess imprisoned in Uz-Talrak, violent furry pygmies and a golem in the Forest of Bones, and a golden dragon. Yet on the return journey, of exactly equal length, the incidence of exciting and interesting events has been practically zero. Doesn't that seem odd to you?"

Dog replaced Sir Edric's empty wine bottle with a full one. "No, sir. Is it not so often the way that thrilling and dangerous quests have a tedious return journey?"

Sir Edric was too busy drinking to reply.

"Besides, you slew all the peril on the way there. There hasn't been enough time for any fresh peril to arrive."

***

When they reached Greenlock a small horde of townspeople rushed to meet them, throwing flowers and cheering their arrival.

Ah, news of my witch-slaying, treasure-rescuing, battle-winning heroism goes before me.

Sir Edric, Dog, Lysandra and the Royal Guards waved to the crowd and rode slowly through the town towards the manor.

They soaked in the adulation, and more than a few fair maidens approached Sir Edric, Dog and the soldiers to warmly express their admiration.

Perhaps I should rest here for a few days...

"The statue!" someone suddenly shouted.

The other peasants all took up the cry and pointed towards a newly sculpted statue that stood proudly on the immaculate front lawn of his manor. Grinning with delight, Sir Edric had Temper burst into a quick trot, and then pulled on the reins to halt his trusty steed. The statue was fantastically realistic, and portrayed a man kneeling in prayer beside a gigantic head in which his sword was buried to the hilt.

Or perhaps not.

The words 'Witchbane and Giant-Killer' had been carved into the base of the statue, and when the others caught up to Sir Edric he heard several Royal Guardsmen sniggering.

Sir Edric paused briefly at his manor to put back the books he had taken and to order some more mirrors for his ceiling. After that he decided it would be selfish to deprive his royal paramour of his presence any longer and rode at a swifter pace, leaving behind Lieutenant Corkwell and the wagons.

"Back at last," he said as he passed through Awyndel's gates. The knight patted Temper on the flank and gave her a congratulatory carrot.

"You've got to see the King at once," Lysandra insisted.

I'd rather see his wife...

"Oh, come now. Surely a little light refreshment and a change of clothes beforehand to ensure I'm in a fit state to be seen would not be amiss?"

The elf brushed a golden lock of hair behind her pointy ear. "No. We're reporting to the King. Come along."

She clicked her tongue and Hamilton's Trousers began to trot away.

Sir Edric sighed, and followed after her. When they reached the outer gate of the castle the guards saluted the sorceress, and when they reached the inner gate Sir Edric and Lysandra dismounted.

"Look after the horses, Dog. Shan't be long."

Unless the King found out about me and his wife after I left, of course.

Inside the castle they had a prolonged wait whilst Lawrence was awakened and informed of their arrival. Sir Edric tapped his toe and opened up his pack to check the royal seals were there.

"Hang on a minute. Isn't it true that whoever holds the royal seals and sceptre is technically the King?" he asked.

Lysandra smiled. "Yes. But if you don't give them to Lawrence I'll roast your nuts."

Ah ha! She might claim to be aloof but now her mind eagerly delves into the contents of my trousers!

Eventually the royal sleepyhead was ready and the two of them were shown into the throne room. As before, Sir Edric noticed Malthus, the Lord Chancellor, was conspicuous by his absence. Lawrence, looking rather groggy, was the only one waiting for them.

Lysandra went down on one knee and averted her eyes. Sir Edric did likewise.

"Get up, get up. I've heard rumours a battle occurred at the Unholy Temple," Lawrence said. He yawned, and continued, "Did you manage to retrieve the seals and sceptre?"

"Indeed, Highness," Sir Edric confirmed, holding up the pack in one hand and the sceptre in the other.

Lawrence beckoned him nearer and he handed over the treasures before returning to stand beside Lysandra.

The King looked inside the pack and breathed a huge sigh of relief.

"Oh, a thousand blessings on you, Sir Edric. How can I ever thank you?"

"I seek no reward, Highness."

He could feel Lysandra giving him a puzzled look, and smiled at her.

Better to have the King owe me a favour than to collect a trinket or title.

"Truly, Sir Edric, you are a noble man. Lysandra, most wise sorceress, tell me all that happened on your journey."

The elf regaled the King with the tremendous tale of their long and perilous journey. She did, however, omit certain parts, such as when Sir Edric mistook her for a prostitute, and when she donned skimpy slave garments in order to rescue Princess Maria. The King gasped in shock to hear that Baron Greymond had been raising the dead, and to learn of Dog's heroism slaying witches and a giant whilst saving his master's life.

"Ah, I met Maria after the Battle of Hornska," Lawrence recalled. "She was such a pretty little thing."

Sir Edric coughed to stop himself laughing out loud.

"So, what happened to Lord Drayton?" the King asked.

He's a slave, and has probably had his knackers chopped off by now. Serves him right, the traitorous, murderous swine.

"Sadly, Highness, we found no sign of him after the battle," Lysandra reported. "He was not killed, and every other captive was recovered. We can only guess that the Ursk devoured him."

King Lawrence frowned. "With Drayton gone I shall need a new lord chamberlain. Someone well-respected, a man of experience and sound judgement. Sir Edric," the King said formally.

Yes! I'll have the King's ear and get paid a fortune for a job even a peasant could do!

"Would you call in to see Lord Pelham and ask him to visit me at his earliest convenience?"

You ungrateful sod.

"I would be honoured, Highness."

***

120

Outside the castle Lysandra bade farewell to Sir Edric and Dog.

"Are you sure you won't have a little drink?" Sir Edric asked. "We've had quite the adventure together, and it would be a fine way to end the journey."

"No, I must return to my fellow mages and tell them what has happened. You're a strange fellow, Sir Edric. I thought you a lusty coward when we first met, yet none can deny it was your wits that saved Maria and your bravery that rescued Lieutenant Corkwell. Perhaps we'll meet again."

"I certainly hope so. Farewell, Lysandra."

"Farewell, Edric."

She strode away, leaving him, Dog and the three horses.

"Off to see your lady friend, sir?" Dog enquired.

It's tempting, but the crowned crumpet probably won't even be out of bed at this hour. Better to get the Pelham nonsense out of the way and attend to business first.

"Yes, but the vixen only comes out to play when it's dark. In the meantime, take the horses back to the house and see they're well looked after, and prepare some food and drink for me. And get any correspondence ready for perusal. The gods alone know what foul material I shall find lurking for me."

Dog bowed obediently and led away Temper, Twenty-Six and Hamilton's Trousers. Sir Edric set off to pay Pelham a quick visit. He knew the lord slightly, having fought alongside him in several battles a decade and more ago. The doorman answered promptly and he was shown in to Pelham's lounge, where the nobleman was slumped in a leather chair. He had a moustache like a walrus and a figure to match.

I pity his horses.

"Good evening, Lord Pelham. I bring glad tidings," Sir Edric greeted the rotund nobleman.

"Is my son-in-law dead?" Pelham asked eagerly.

"Well, not *that* glad," Sir Edric admitted. "Lord Drayton is missing, presumed lunch, and in his infinite wisdom our glorious monarch has named you the new lord chamberlain."

The spherical lord was silent, and his moustache drooped at the news.

He seems unexpectedly downcast. Probably depressed at having to spend so much time with Lawrence.

"Something wrong?"

Lord Pelham sighed. "Yes. Would you like a drink?"

Over the course of several bottles of wine the truth emerged. Pelham was well aware of the political machinations of Malthus and his ilk, and bone idle to boot. The role of lord chamberlain, whilst immensely powerful, also brought with it enemies and obligations, and the elderly lord was far happier in retirement.

"I've served the kingdom all my life. A chap's entitled to easy living when he reaches my age," Pelham asserted.

"Indeed," Sir Edric agreed. "Might I ask how old you are?"

"Fifty-one."

...it's not that old.

"All I want is a bit of ease and comfort. Tell the King to piss off!" he exclaimed with drunken defiance.

Sir Edric grinned. "Sure you want me to use those precise words?"

Pelham frowned, and his moustache wobbled with uncertainty. "Er, no. Make something up, Edric. You've a sharp mind. Tell him I'm ill, or I've become a hermit. Recommend yourself for the job if you want it."

Huzzah for the walrus lord!

"Oh, I'm sure there are more capable men than I."

Although one of them is presently the slave of a vicious matriarch.

"But you will tell the King I can't do it?" Pelham asked.

Sir Edric put down his glass of wine. "Of course I'd like to help you, Lord Pelham, but the King did command it. Lying to the monarch is a serious matter."

Pelham sighed. "Wait here."

The hippopotamus plodded out of the room and returned a short while later with a tiny silk purse which he tossed to the knight.

This is disappointingly small...

He tipped out the contents and was delighted to see little rubies and emeralds spill into his hands.

"Terribly sorry to hear of your tragic illness, Lord Pelham. I can see it is the will of the gods that another man become lord chamberlain."

"Thank you, Sir Edric. I knew a man of your piety would understand."

It was still a bright sunny day when he emerged from Pelham's palatial residence, and he strolled towards his rather more modest abode.

With all these jewels and Boris' bounty I should perhaps find myself a more fitting home. Something with towers. And a moat.

Upon reaching his house he immediately went to see his horses. After satisfying himself that the stable hands did not deserve a thrashing he went inside and seated himself at the dining table. Dog had prepared quite the spread. Beef, mutton, venison, chicken, goose, swan, snake, bear, boar and pork vied for room with the bottles of beer and wine.

"Where's the whisky?" he asked indignantly. "I'm not a bloody peasant, Dog. Honestly."

There had been no whisky left in the house, Sir Edric discovered, and so he sent his manservant scurrying off to buy some more. Whilst Dog was gone Sir Edric began to tuck into the meal, well aware that he would need all his strength for the nocturnal exertions ahead. The seat next to his own was occupied by a small and tidy pile of correspondence that his manservant had gathered. When Dog returned with the whisky his master waved his knife at the letters. Dog moved to obey, so that Sir Edric could sort through the epistles without breaking away from his meal.

"This appears to be a blood seal from an Ursk," Dog observed of the uppermost letter.

Gods, please don't be from Grog.

"Open it, and see who it's from," Sir Edric commanded before draining dry a wine vessel.

"Ah, Orff No-Balsac, sir," Dog said, smiling.

Huzzah!

"He sends a gracious thank you for your assistance regarding Lysandra, and assures you that Bellman has been suitably disposed of. Oh, and he has a business proposition for you at your earliest convenience."

Several other letters were from his vassals, and Sir Edric directed Dog to attend to them when he had the time. One bore the seal of Esmerelda and he had Dog throw the damned thing in the fire before its evil infected the house. The final letter was of most interest.

"It is emblazoned with the crest of Matriarch Vellia, sir. Ought I open it?"

"No, hand it here at once."

Dog did so, and Sir Edric neatly sliced it open with his knife. He unfolded the letter and laughed.

"Vellia confirms receipt of my gift. Poor Drayton. She's renamed him Lomar, and fitted him with a collar so he can't leave the Blue Forest. Super." He wiped his mouth clean with a napkin and rose from his seat. "The time has come for me to re-establish royal relations. Get the fire stoked in my room for when I return, Dog."

"Yes, sir."

Sir Edric handed the letter from Matriarch Vellia to his servant. "And find a frame for this."

He left his house and strode off to find the frisky vixen. After spending so much time riding it felt a little strange to be wandering about on foot, but he was confident that the journey had reinvigorated him. He was eager to see her once more. Like an overcast sky he was just about ready to burst.

She kept a town house that few knew of, and there was a secret entrance round the back. Sir Edric had to rummage around for a moment or two, for it was entirely dark and he couldn't see what he was fiddling with, but eventually he managed to enter the back door. Flickering candlelight beneath the bedroom door suggested she was both in and awake, and he was about to walk in when he heard a girlish giggling followed by a man's voice.

"I heard a rumour that Edric's come back," the man said.

I know that voice… it's Jeremy Holbrook!

"I don't care," she replied.

You treacherous bitch!

"He left without so much as a word. Besides, you're much more vigorous than that old man ever was."

Jeremy laughed. "That's true. If he ventures to return I'll cut the coward to pieces."

Sir Edric reached into his quiver for a crossbow bolt, and found to his chagrin that both the weapon and its ammunition were still at his home. For the first time in over a month he was without his beloved weapon, and although he was tempted to charge in and murder Jeremy that would create the problem of a royal witness.

Damn the pair of them!

Reluctantly he slinked away, making certain to be as quiet as a mouse in slippers. Once free of the lusty harlot's home he made for the nearest tavern, threw a quantity of money in the direction of the barkeep and began to drown his sorrows.

"Bad day?" someone asked him.

Mind your own business, you nosy-

"Corkwell?" he asked in surprise. "When did you get back?"

She helped herself to his beer, then thumped the tankard on the bar and clicked her fingers to summon the barkeep. "Fill this up and get me one too." The lieutenant turned back to Sir Edric. "Just now. The King was whining about Drayton's capture." Corkwell laughed. "He threatened to demote me, but given half the Royal Guards ended up dead he can't afford to lose me. Ungrateful sod."

"I'm beginning to go off our royal couple," Sir Edric confessed, drinking his beer and sighing.

"The slut's shacked up with someone else has she?"

"Indeed," he glumly replied. "But the night is yet young. We could have a few more drinks, and then catch up on old times."

Corkwell frowned, and sipped her beer. "I'm afraid not. After this beer I have plans."

It was worth a try...

"Most of them involve you, some manacles, and a riding crop."

***

A knocking at his door announced the arrival of Dog, and, more importantly, breakfast. Sir Edric shouted for him to enter, and the manservant came in. He carried a tray filled with toast, eggs, jam, marmalade, biscuits, bacon, wine and beer.

Thank the gods, it's been weeks since I've had a proper breakfast.

Whilst the knight set about attacking the copious quantity of food, his manservant began laying out his master's clothes for the day ahead.

"Did you hear about the Queen, sir?" Dog enquired as he folded an undershirt and placed it on the dressing table.

"No," Sir Edric mumbled through a mouthful of half-chewed bacon.

"The King sent the Royal Guard to her townhouse, unannounced. They caught her in an act of intimacy with Sir

Jeremy Holbrook, who was summarily executed. The Queen herself was divorced at once and packed off to a nunnery."

Those lucky nuns...

"Gosh, how unfortunate."

Dog brushed a speck of dirt off of the trousers he had selected. "The rumour is, sir, that someone tipped off the King about his wife's... indiscretions."

"Shocking, Dog, simply shocking. You can't trust anyone these days."

"Indeed, sir."

Acknowledgements

First and foremost, I'd like to thank the people who bought this book (and previous ones, as they didn't have acknowledgement sections). I hope you enjoyed reading it as much as I enjoyed writing it. If you did, please consider rating, reviewing and recommending it. As a self-published author writing and publishing a book is a walk in the park compared to getting a good profile, so this really would help and be greatly appreciated.

This is my first comedy, and also the first book I've written which has been extensively beta read. The feedback, suggestions and honest critiquing of my quartet of beta readers has proved invaluable (hopefully you agree, given this bit's at the back of the book and you've probably read the whole thing).

In order of volunteering, Jo Zebedee, Prizzley, Moonbat and J Scott Marryat have provided much needed reassurance regarding the comedy (it's sometimes hard to judge if a joke's funny when you've read it 7 times and any sense of novelty has evaporated), pointed out inconsistencies or just highlighted where a lack of clarity was getting in the way. Many thanks to all of them for their kind assistance.

For my three books (including this one) to date I've been fortunate in my cover artist, Yoong. Not only has she put together three great covers, she's also been very easy to work with (and patient with my inartistic mindset).

Last but not least, many thanks to Mr. Llama, for his continual encouragement/kicks up the arse. Writing's a mostly solitary business, as you'd expect, and it's nice to hear when someone's looking forward to the next book.

About the Author

Thaddeus White is the pen name for someone else. Aside from the strange awkwardness of the third person he has always enjoyed writing, as well as reading (mostly classical history and fantasy of late). At present he is working on a trilogy about the civil war in Denland (this takes places in the Bane of Souls/Journey to Altmortis world, which is entirely separate to the realm which Sir Edric occupies).

In addition, he hopes to write more of Sir Edric's misadventures, and has vague, fuzzy plans for another stand-alone fantasy in the Bane of Souls/Journey to Altmortis world.

For those interested in learning more about the world of Bane of Souls/Journey to Altmortis and what the author is presently writing, please visit his website at: http://thaddeuswhite.weebly.com

For rambly book reviews and occasional witterings on TV, films, videogames and classical history, visit http://thaddeusthesixth.blogspot.com/

If you're on Twitter, your praise, criticism, and devotional haikus are all welcome at: https://twitter.com/MorrisF1